DOLPHINS
A WING

DOLPHINS A WING

MICHELE ETHIER

DOLPHINS A WING

iUniverse books may be ordered through booksellers or by contacting:

iUniverse
1663 Liberty Drive
Bloomington, IN 47403
www.iuniverse.com
1-800-Authors (1-800-288-4677)

ISBN: 978-1-5320-5915-5 (sc)
ISBN: 978-1-5320-5914-8 (hc)
ISBN: 978-1-5320-5916-2 (e)

Library of Congress Control Number: 2018912126

Print information available on the last page.

iUniverse rev. date: 10/26/2018

Author's Note

My dilemma was where to start? Our story began before we ever realized that we were drawing energy from our past lives together, let alone our realities in the present. We all just knew in our hearts we belonged to one another and would always be true friends. I am certain that our bond began in lifetimes long before this one. I don't want to confuse you with this train of thought. What I am describing is a group of women who have loved one another deeply since the beginning of time. This is my belief, and this is my story.

Our present lifetime is where my story takes place. It involves my sisterhood, my group of lifelong friends who have supported one another wholeheartedly and with unconditional love. Each day I bow my head in gratitude for how fortunate and blessed my life has been. I am so thankful for my family, friends, husband, children, and so much else. My life has been an amazing kaleidoscope of color. And who could argue against a life filled with such a variety of colors, shapes, and textures? You can't.

It's everywhere—colorful language, colorful flowers, colorful seasons that change as the minutes and hours and days flow by, always presenting something completely new and different from any other season you've ever known. My experiences in life have allowed me to truly see the importance of taking in every beautiful moment we have. Despite the times of pain, confusion, heartbreak, or disappointment, including my stroke a few years ago, life has always been a blessing for me.

More than once people have told me, "Wow, you live under a lucky star!" Since I was a little girl, I have always wished on shooting stars whenever I've seen them dart across the sky, nearly all my wishes have come true. When I was ten years old, I began wishing for a pony, and before long, some family friends at a nearby dude ranch gave me a beautiful golden Shetland pony. That was enough to convince me that if I wished fervently enough and truly believed, my wishes would come true. And it worked—every single time.

My wish now is that through these pages you are able to share with me in the colorful beauty of this sisterhood and the joy of true friendship. As you relate to any part of this story about the love and laughter among daughters, sisters, mothers, grandmothers, and best friends, I hope to send you a special aha moment. Take that moment to pause and think about those people and/or animals you have chosen to surround yourself with in this lifetime. Acknowledge the powerful men and women in your life. There is no need for jealousy, mistrust, or anger toward them. We are here because of them. Our relationships with these special souls have molded us into who we are today, and they have been with us throughout lifetimes. Go hug your grandmother today if you are lucky enough to have one still living. Hug your mother, your daughters, your sisters, and your friends. If you can't give a physical hug, give them a call. Send them a card, an email, or even a text to thank them for being such important parts of your life.

Each morning before getting out of bed, I ask for divine guidance, especially from female energies, for strength to walk in grace and to do at least one thing that will make another person smile. Maybe I don't always make someone smile, but at least I smile from within for trying.

Today I wish to share my story with you. For many years I have kept this experience in my heart, written it on napkins and in numerous diaries. When I've shared it, people are always amazed by the hysterical happenings my friends and I encountered at our angel-and-dolphin retreat, and more than a few of them have encouraged me to write down my story—a notion that has finally become a reality.

This is the story of a vacation I took with five of my most cherished girlfriends. I have changed the names to protect the innocent, and, believe me, they really are innocent. I may remember some aspects that are altogether different from what they may recall. As it has flowed from my mind onto paper, my *true* story has taken on a life of its own, and as the author, I have taken the liberty of making a few small embellishments. Therefore, this book blends nonfiction with a touch of fantasy, depending on the chapter you are reading. This book is about experiences. Every experience is a gift, whether sad or happy. My advice is that you embrace each of your experiences and learn from them. They are leading you toward discovering who *you* really are.

Special dedication to my "guardian Angels"

Lorna
Janice
Margarethe
Stephanye
Joni
Deenie
Glen
SaiMoon

ACKNOWLEDGMENTS

Every single person who has entered my life, has in some way given to my heart in positive ways and thus assisted in shaping my words and the telling of my stories. Thank you. Without relationships we have built together, I wouldn't be the woman I am today.

My deepest, heartfelt gratitude is humbly given to my editors, Megan Rivera and John Thompson.

I always wondered why authors would lavish endless amounts of praise upon their editors. I understand now, why that is. I handed them a box of tangled sentences and words, similar to a box of tangled and knotted Christmas tree lights. They would patiently string my thoughts and words into the beautiful story I meant to tell. I don't know how they do it, but they would repeatedly remind me, "There are writers and there are editors" Thank God for that simple truth.

Of course I must thank my dearest friends for reminding me how much I cherish our friendships, and enduring my 'story telling' with love and understanding.

Lastly (but never least): to Craig, Laef, Koll and Bryn who continue to make me feel like the richest and luckiest woman on the planet.

1

When Layne and I saw the brochure on the bulletin board at Unity Church, I knew I was in! The big bold letters called loudly to me. *Swim with Wild Dolphins! Connect with Your Spiritual Angel Guides!* I knew instantly that I could convince Layne and our other lifelong friends to join me.

At the time, I was nearly thirty-nine years old. I had a wonderful, nearly perfect husband (seriously, he was nearly perfect) and three reasonably normal children. For many years I'd been a stay-at-home mom, but had recently decided to go back to work three days a week. I took a part-time job at a local hospital, admitting patients into the ER. One day a week, I also worked as a surgical consultant and technician to a prominent plastic surgeon. All in all, life seemed perfect. Life was perfect.

MaryAnn, my older sister, had convinced me to go back to work. An ER charge nurse at the hospital, she would occasionally drop by our ranch-style house for lunch. She is a Capricorn and a take-charge lady. During our childhood, she was my idol, helping manage our household and supervising all of us five younger siblings. When my children were in elementary school, junior high, and high school, our house was always filled with kids swimming in the pool, playing billiards, or riding our horses. Fortunately, I had learned from MaryAnn how to be the one taking care and taking charge.

During one of these lunch visits, my sister convinced me to return to the workforce. Out of the blue, she said she could get me a part-time job in the ER—something I had once dreamed of doing. But I'd been out of the game for so long. I looked at her as if she were crazy. "No, no, no, I don't need to work," I said, shaking my head in protest as I reached for more laundry from the huge pile of clothes mounted on the kitchen table. But as soon as the words crossed my lips, I looked outside at a plate that had once been filled with nachos. They'd been greedily consumed by my kids and their friends, and now one of our three dogs was licking the plate clean. At the same time, I realized I was tapping my foot to a song I had heard at least a hundred times, played by the band that was practicing in the living room. (Our eldest son was the drummer.) Suddenly, I thought, *Hell, yeah! I would probably enjoy going back to work again.*

I had left my profession in the medical/dental field years earlier to stay home and raise our babies. I loved being a wife and a mom. And I felt so blessed to be free of responsibilities outside of caring for our children. I can definitely say that motherhood during those early years was the best period of my life—so far. My husband was a dream, the best man any woman could ever ask for. We met when I was nineteen years old. I can still remember my mother's words of wisdom: "Marry a doctor, a dentist, or a lawyer." I'm not sure, but her motherly advice may have subconsciously led me to Craig, a wonderful Norwegian man just out of dental school who simply stole my heart. I was smitten with his honesty, integrity, good looks, and witty personality. Those were the same feelings I'd had for Paul McCartney when I was in the fourth grade. It was out-of-control, heart-throbbing madness. I had found my Prince Charming.

It seemed to me that my husband was so very smart. I hung on his every word and vowed to love him forever. Many of my friends started calling him Saint Craig because he seemed so perfect. But that impression changed slightly once our children became teenagers and were able to google everything their dad claimed to know. Suddenly, he became Dr. Know-It-All. Google didn't exist during our dating years. Now that it did, I had to admit that I started looking at Craig in a different light—a light that was still bright but not quite as bright as it had once been.

About a week after coming across the brochure about swimming with dolphins, Layne and I made plans to meet up for walk. I awoke that morning and quickly began my daily chores. After feeding the horses, goats, chickens, and pony, I put them out in the pasture. I then cleaned the stalls and gave them fresh water, and I decided to put off pruning my rose gardens until later. My spirit was embracing the brisk autumn breeze, reveling in the golds and vivid oranges of the changing leaves surrounding our home. With all my morning chores finished, I saddled up Sai Moon, my white Arabian, for a ride through the evergreen forest, which was like a canopy surrounding our home, and then I went to meet up with Layne.

I had owned Sai Moon since he was a weanling. Throughout the years we had shared countless hours of excitement and triumph in local and national horse shows. Though he was normally bouncing with energy, today he was calm, taking in the quiet beauty of the tall firs and yellow leaves carpeting the trails. As we rode, the wind whispered, "Good morning," which caused a single leaf to fall from the trees and sent a ripple of joy through Sai Moon, who began to lightly prance. At times, when riding him, I felt like I was sitting upon a cloud. Over time he and I had become like one, able to feel the happiness coursing through each other's veins during our frequent rides.

Before long, I was able to make out Layne's tall frame and long raven-colored hair in the distance. We had been close friends since our children were small. A truly spiritual soul, she lived and talked in a different realm from that of most *normal* human beings. But she and I had always shared a connection. We simply adored each other. She'd overcome so much heartache in her life—children, substance abuse, marriages, the death of a spouse. All these experiences had given her the unique ability to always find peace and serenity amid the ups and downs of life. She also had a clairvoyance that enabled her to talk with beings from the other side, including her grandmothers. I loved and respected her tremendously.

"Morning, Misha!" Layne called out when she saw me. A glorious smile spread across her beautiful face as she waved. As we walked along, enjoying the crisp morning together, it wasn't long before the brochure from the previous week crept into our conversation. Even though the two week excursion wasn't happening until mid-January, we were already reflecting on how awesome it would be to unwind with our friends at the retreat, escaping our hectic lives, especially, following the postholiday season. We both felt deeply intrigued and knew in our heart of hearts that this retreat would be something uniquely special.

"Christmas at our house is over the top," I mentioned to her. "My daughter says I decorate the house like a gay queen smoking crack! I just do it because I want this time of year to feel special for the kids, but truthfully, I always feel a little burned out and frayed at the edges by the end of it. We should get all the girls to go with us. I'm sure we can convince them all to come along. Even if we don't get to swim with the wild dolphins, we can at least ride on the gossamer wings of our angels!"

Layne and I giggled and then started making the plans to attend this retreat with our friends.

2

As I rode back toward home, a ripple of excitement coursed through me. I knew I needed space in my mind and life—from caring for three children, a husband, an aging father, horses, ponies, goats, chickens, three dogs, four cats, a variety of fish, gardens, fruit trees, not to mention my new job. I had also been caring for my mother during her graceful, heroic battle with Lou Gehrig's disease. She had passed away in my arms. In some ways I felt as though my life had never actually been my own. I had always allowed it to belong to my loved ones. At the very beginning of motherhood, I realized that my life was indeed *not* my own. It belonged to *them*. I believed and trusted that this was as it should be.

Growing up, I'd always felt this need to make everyone happy. Middle-child syndrome, I'd been told. I'd had a traditional Catholic upbringing and thought of myself as the *lost child* in the middle. At an early age, I figured out that what worked best for me and everybody else was to just get along and be happy. I was the peacemaker in the middle of a chaotic family of eight. I knew we just needed to love one another. So with my positive attitude and outlook on life, that was exactly what I did.

I believe the most important influence of my childhood was my dad's never-ending embrace of music and poetry. He would play the piano, and we would all sing along with the lyrics he wrote. When I was five years old, I loved performing for my parents' friends. Pretending that I was Shirley Temple, I would stand on the piano and sing. In addition to his musical talents, writing poetry, writing songs, playing the piano, and singing, Dad was also a stand-up comedian, and I drew as much as I could from his well. Eventually, he became the creative director for several prestigious advertising companies in the Pacific Northwest. Known as "the Adman," he not only composed countless jingles but also played the music while producing and directing all of them. Dad was my hero, and I was certain he hung the moon and placed all the stars in the sky. He went on to win a number of international Clio Awards, which are the radio broadcasting equivalent of the Oscars.

While I inherited creativity from my dad, I received tenacity and a love of cleaning, fashion flair, gardening, and organizing (sounds boring, huh?) from my mother. Her strength and solid German heritage were crucial factors in my becoming the woman I am today. Mom's strength in character and determination were boundless. As Dad and I cared for Mom the last year of her life, it was sad to see this powerhouse woman shrink in demeanor and size before our eyes. It took all the strength and courage we could muster. But in hindsight she was the one with the strength and courage. Mom died gracefully and peacefully in our arms with Dad cradling her head and me holding her hand. One of my sisters held her other hand, while my other two sisters held her legs and feet. Our tears were the river she floated on all the way to heaven. I hope that when I leave this earth, I will be surrounded and held by my loved ones as tenderly as my mother was.

Mom and Dad had already had the six of us kids before they were thirty. My dad had literally pleaded with the church to let him use birth control or get a vasectomy, but that's another story. My mother didn't discover who she really was until we all had grown up and moved away. It was only after becoming a grandma, suffering a nervous breakdown, and being taken away in a straitjacket that she finally quit smoking two packs of cigarettes a day and backed off on her martini hour. The yelling, hitting, mean, and rigid *Mommy Dearest* from my childhood finally melted into a woman of mellow tolerance who started to do something she had rarely done before. She started to laugh … a lot! After retiring from her stressful career in corporate management, she became an understanding, tender, and patient grandmother. She was a completely different woman from the mom I knew growing up. I shook my head in wonder and sadness as it dawned on me that having six children in her twenties was what had made her so angry.

Craig and I had been married for many years, and I needed a break. We had a six-year-old daughter with two brothers, who were wonderful young teenagers—though that seems like an oxymoron to say—and their mood swings were taking a toll on me. I thought toddlers and preteens were difficult, but teenagers put a whole different perspective on parenting. Going back to work had also been much more stressful than I'd imagined or anticipated. I'd had to learn how to type again, this time on a computer. Talk about teaching an old dog new tricks! At the hospital I was admitting injured patients into the ER, and I'd been under pressure to learn all kinds of new tricks fast. Several times when I wasn't fast enough, I ended up with blood-soaked papers all over my desk. I often felt exhausted by the new challenges. And now that my children were teenagers, I felt I had lost my babies. Maybe I had lost myself.

Like my mom, I had never really *found* myself before my babies arrived. Now that she was gone, I missed her terribly, and I found myself wishing that we could have shared more of this lifetime together. Maybe this Hawaiian retreat with swimming with dolphins and reaching out to my guardian angels would help me find myself and grow closer to my late mother.

Immediately after returning home from my ride with Layne, I put Sai Moon in the stables and then called each of my closest girlfriends to invite them to an informational presentation on the angel and dolphin retreat. All of them agreed to attend. Since several of us knew the pastor at Unity Church, we immediately trusted what the church seemed to be endorsing. We learned better later.

The presentation enticed us with its cleansing promises of organic foods, guardian angels, and swimming with wild dolphins. Who wouldn't want to swim with wild dolphins? We learned that the retreat facility was strategically located near a bay that was densely inhabited by spinner dolphins. In fact, this bay was the most watched and studied by scientists from around the world because of the spinner dolphins that passed through by the hundreds of thousands.

When we huddled together after the presentation, my best friends—Layne, Jeanne, Kat, Torey, and Ziggy—all agreed to go. We all knew we could use a tropical vacation after the holiday season's overindulgences—sun, swimming, healthy food, exercise, yoga, meditation, relaxing in a tropical paradise. We needed a truly spiritual retreat. It really didn't take much to convince us. We didn't even complain about the no-alcohol-and-no-drugs provision. We were all in our late thirties or early forties, and we were all divorcée, mothers, and businesswomen. Had we reached our pinnacles in our lives? What else was out there?

The girls seemed just as enthusiastic about the trip as I was. There was Layne, a sister, daughter, mother, and grandmother since time began. With long black hair and sparkling, intensely blue eyes, she was the tallest member of our group. The first of us to have children, she was a published author and our spiritual guide. Divorced, married, divorced, engaged—she seemed to have men fawning over her at all times. In my opinion, she was lucky to be falling in love at every corner of her life. Much heartache and heartbreak came with the territory, but lessons learned in life were embedded deep within her heart. I deeply admired her knowledge of life. She was truly an old and very wise soul.

Then there was Kat, an extremely successful real estate agent, a divorcée, mother of two lovely grown daughters, and grandmother to two grandchildren. She was a beautiful, natural blonde with a gorgeous, toned figure that she maintained by going to the gym on a regular basis. Poised, elegant, and classy, she had a knack for always seeing the best in any situation.

Our little Torey worked as a financial planner, stockbroker, and insurance agent. She did her best to control everything she was involved in with total confidence and much aplomb, which was reflected in her career choices and perhaps made up for her lack of height. A stocky brunette with henna-red highlights and a dynamo personality, she stood nearly five feet tall. We'd been close friends since kindergarten, and she was completely steadfast in her loyalty to her friends. Torey's whiskey-and-honey-colored eyes crinkled in the corners when she smiled, which was often. She had never been married, but she always said that she was keeping her eyes and arms wide open for that special man.

Next there was Ziggy. She and I had become close friends

when my daughter was two years old. She owned her own hair salon, had been divorced twice, and had a son in grade school. Artistic, creative, and wise beyond her years, Ziggy was a petite strawberry blonde with an infectious personality and a great sense of humor. As the youngest of our group, she had the most gorgeous smile and body. She had a sophisticated wit that could captivate anyone, and her hershey's chocolate, golden eyes danced with merriment at every turn.

Last but certainly not least was Jeanne, who had been my best friend since junior high. She was a successful rep for a Canadian textile company, twice a divorcée, and the mother of two grown children. Although a little on the heavy side during this particular time in her life, Jeanne and I were nearly carbon copies of each other. I had long blonde hair and bright blue eyes though, while Jeanne had long red hair and emerald-green cat eyes that were speckled with gold-and-rust-colored flecks much like the copper-colored freckles all over her body. I loved Jeanne's eyes! They were her most captivating feature. A true redhead with a zest for life and wit that wouldn't quit, Jeanne was also quite the caretaker. She was our mother hen, keeping the flock together. Jeanne was my personal angel on earth, and on countless occasions over the years, I've had to catch my breath in wonder at how blessed we were to have such an effortless friendship. I loved her dearly from the first day we met.

And, of course, there was me. I wasn't very tall, and my hair was blonde ... or sandy brown ... or red ... or mahogany, depending on the seasons and my mood. My legs were usually a bit stocky, but at that time they were looking pretty good, as I was eight weeks postop from liposuction (one of the benefits of working with a plastic surgeon). I am outgoing, almost always in a good mood, and a genuine people pleaser and would give any one of these ladies the shirt off my back. Oh, did I mention I am a big enabler who wants the whole world or at least the people around me to be happy and live fulfilling lives? That was why our six-bedroom ranch-style house was never empty. When one child left, another showed up. Friends of mine and friends of our children would move in, live with us, and grow to become close friends of our whole family.

Always the mama bear, Jeanne had taken it upon herself to handle all our reservations for the plane and rental cars. She even arranged for a white stretch limo to pick us up and take us to the airport. Jeanne picked me up first, and we immediately popped a bottle of champagne. Well, there went the no-alcohol rule, at least for now.

Next we picked up Torey, who was a little miffed because she had expected to be picked up last and wasn't quite ready yet. All her luggage was waiting outside in the driveway minus her cosmetics bag. She had planned to paint her toenails before leaving, but she hadn't had the time to apply the bubblegum pink polish. We were scrambling to help her avoid a meltdown.

After calming Torey down, we rolled over to pick up Kat. That was when Torey noticed that her bags weren't in the limo. We could picture them sitting in the driveway, except for her cosmetic bag, which was sitting on her front porch, where she had placed it while locking up. We made a U-turn back to Torey's house. After driving all the way back to Torey's house, we climbed out of the limo to help load up her bags. That was when we heard it—a soft, nonstop humming. We looked around. What was that? Where was it coming from? Suddenly, Torey laughed as she opened one of her bags to reveal her vibrator! I told her she probably wouldn't need it. We would be sharing rooms and that might not be something she would want to share with us.

"Speak for yourself, married lady," said Jeanne. We

laughed, and I admitted that the sleek black toy actually looked pretty enticing.

When we arrived at Ziggy's, she was waiting impatiently on her front door step. We were all together at last, embracing the adventure before us. Layne was the only one not with us. She had taken an earlier flight so she could begin working in the kitchen and garden at the retreat. A little strapped for cash, she'd jumped on the chance to work at the retreat in exchange for her stay.

On the way to the airport, we slammed two bottles of champagne between the five of us. Then at the airport, agreeing we were still in holiday mode, we each slugged a Bloody Mary. We were going to be in a no-alcohol environment soon, so why not celebrate now? There was nothing wrong with us toasting to simply being alive, being happy, and being together and one with the world. Healthy food, finding our guardian angels, and swimming with wild dolphins were all just around the corner.

The fun continued on board as the flight attendant in first-class kept the champagne flowing. I later learned that my husband had called in a favor from a dear friend of ours who worked for the airline. She'd been my roommate after high school when Craig and I started dating. He'd asked her to make our flight the best it could be, so she'd used her connections to make sure we received an endless supply of champagne. By the time our plane landed in Hawaii, we were all hammered and ready to rock and roll!

Jeanne had volunteered to be our designated driver upon arrival, so she abstained from drinking too much. Right after boarding, she'd taken a shot of NyQuil, saying she felt a cold coming on, and then she slept peacefully the whole flight. As soon as we arrived on the big island of Hawaii, Jeanne went to pick up our rental van. Kat, Torey, Ziggy, and I weren't excited about driving, and I also had no sense of direction.

After filling the van with our luggage, we were off. Full of laughter and ready to take on the world, we couldn't wait to meet our angels and swim with wild dolphins. We were driving happily toward the slowly sinking sun when Jeanne abruptly pulled into a liquor store parking lot. We fell silent.

"Um ... maybe we should grab some water?" Kat suggested half-heartedly.

"No alcohol," I firmly reminded everyone. "If we can't do this, we are all losers!"

Jeanne turned around in her seat. "Okay, this is our last chance because the next stop is prison. So who wants piña coladas and mai tais?"

"I'm a big fat *loser*!" Ziggy exclaimed as she slid the rolling door open.

It didn't take us more than a few seconds to pile out of the van and head into the liquor store. We each got our own cart and piled in our drinks of choice. I picked up fifths of tequila, gin, Kahlúa, rum, and vodka. Kat had her own fifths of rum, vodka, brandy, and cognac along with two bottles of white wine and four bottles of red wine. What a classy lady. Torey had vodka and six bottles of red wine. Ziggy had rum and assorted mixers. At the checkout, Jeanne showed up with half gallons of all the above. We couldn't contain the peels of hysterical laughter. In the first of many powwows over the course of our trip, we joined together, our arms interlaced and heads together, gasping for air in between bursts of laughter.

Finally, after an intense discussion, we agreed to just buy the supersized half gallons of everything. When we stopped at a grocery store for cups and other assorted goodies, we actually refrained from purchasing any junk food, but only because I put all the bad foods back on the shelves and gave everybody a pep talk about how this was supposed to be a cleansing trip. Alcohol was our only digression, except that

I couldn't resist buying five Styrofoam noodles, those things people floated with in the pool. And they had horse heads on one end! When we were done shopping, we stuffed ourselves back into the van and rode our Styrofoam horses to our final destination. Eventually, we had to sit on our horses because Kat started playfully hitting everyone on the head with them. Already enjoying ourselves immensely, we were growing more wild and free with each turn. With the windows down and our hair flying in the wind, we sang along loudly with every song on the radio.

"Decibel level down!" Jeanne suddenly shouted from the driver's seat. "Everybody, shut up right now! You're acting like a bunch of kids! We're getting close, and I need help finding this place. And I need a drink!" Jeanne had refrained from drinking much on the plane, knowing she was going to be driving upon our arrival.

Torey was feeling anxious because we were going to be late for the opening spiritual ceremony. She also still needed to put polish on her toenails as she reminded us for the third time since leaving that morning. It was so unlike her not to be perfectly put together right down to her toes. Stress and Torey didn't mix well, but she always seemed to find herself in it. The world just wasn't organized enough for her, but she was always trying to make it so. She didn't have children and had never been married, so she hadn't had to deal with the unpredictability of a child or the compromise of marriage. Possibly because of this, her coping skills weren't as mature as the rest of ours. But she sure had her act together in her financial planning business. I laughed as I thought about my tightly wound little Torey, my friends' background laughter dancing in my ears.

3

This part of Hawaii was all black lava rock, and in many places it looked like we'd landed on the moon. For me, the unexpected combination of the black lava rocks with the lush green trees and vibrant flowers was mind altering. It reminded me that friendships like ours were beyond words. It was as if we'd all merged into one entity, the same way the lava rocks and foliage melded into this beautiful paradise. All was well within our world. We had left our everyday lives in what felt like the distant past, healthy relaxation and meditation shining brightly in our futures, or so I thought.

When we pulled up to our destination, we were met by an enormous woman in a blue muumuu imprinted with orange-and-red hibiscus flowers who was blocking the middle of the road. She was morbidly obese with a puffy grayish pallor to her face. Her hair looked like it might have once been blonde, but now it was gray, thin, stringy, and patchy in spots. She was sweating profusely in the late afternoon humidity. Her gargantuan frame was firmly planted in the roadway, legs splayed in a wide-open stance as she motioned toward the place where we were to park while simultaneously berating us for being late.

"Don't park there!" the woman barked angrily as she waved her huge arm, causing the giant slab of wobbling fat that was her underarm to swing like a pendulum. "Over here! Now! Don't stir up too much dust! Drive slowly! Park here at an angle! *Stop!*"

Twisting in her seat, Jeanne looked at each of us in turn. "Who the hell is this bitch?" she asked under her breath.

Appalled by the woman's lack of courtesy and professionalism, I wondered if we were in the right place. Whoever this woman was, unfortunately, she seemed to be the one in control. Once Jeanne had obediently parked, the woman ordered us to bring our belongings to our rooms immediately and then check back in with her for our purifying salt scrubs. This woman's abrasive welcome had burst our bubbles, and we got out of the van like dogs with their tails between their legs.

As we unpacked the van, we whispered among ourselves, trying not to laugh. Holding back the giggles required superhuman control, especially when we made eye contact. Her hands on her hips, the woman stood there glaring at us. "Which one of you is Misha?" she asked in a firm, hushed voice. Uh-oh. I remained mute, but Torey pointed her tiny finger directly at me. "I'm Reverend Faith, your retreat leader," she said, handing me a bunch of necklaces with name tags that looked like something I would have worn in kindergarten. They were nothing more than laminated index cards with colored yarn threaded through the hole-punched corners. "Pass these out, and don't forget that when you leave your rooms for meal breaks, you *must* be wearing these at all times. If anyone loses a name tag, you have to pay for a new one."

"Can I have a different color yarn?" Ziggy asked. "I don't like red."

"You will learn to love it and everything else in your life by the time you leave," the reverend replied with a strained smile. *Well then*, I thought, *maybe this harsh greeting is all a technique to help us prepare to meet our spiritual angel guides and unite us with the dolphins.*

"Um, is there anyone who can help take my luggage up to the room?" Torey, the shortest and the most entitled of our group, asked. I instantly knew that it was the wrong thing to ask.

"Yeah, that would be awesome. We brought a lot of stuff," Kat echoed.

The reverend calmly answered with the same strained smile on her face. "Ladies, you're on your own in that department. Just walk down this path, and you will see our grass hut. Go up the stairs, and your rooms are the two on the left. Since there are five of you, three will share one room, and the other two will share the adjoining room. When you reach the top of the stairs, you will see our sacred ceremony circle, which is defined by a circle of white rice. *Do not*—I repeat *do not*—touch or enter the sacred circle. It is protected by our sacred angel guides and has been purified for us to enter later this evening. We have rules here that everyone must abide by, or else the dolphins won't come for us when it is our time to swim and play with them."

"I need to pee and do my toenails," Torey whispered as we gathered our suitcases. "Come on. Let's get shaking."

With her hands on her wide hips, the woman continued to watch us as we set off down the path toward our hut. The grounds were not groomed or well maintained. Everything was junglelike. The trees were shrouded in plumeria, while bougainvillea stretched their tall, swirling vines up toward the blue sky as if reaching for the sun. I inhaled the wonderful, ripe smells of the papayas, mangos, and avocados that dangled from the nearby trees. Birds of paradise stood tall like soldiers along the walkway as if to salute our arrival. As I tuned into the harmonious, tropical birdsongs around us, I could vaguely hear the sound of the crashing surf in the distance.

Eventually, our living quarters emerged from among a jungle of lush wildness. A beautiful vine-covered lanai completely surrounded our circular Hawaiian hut. Well, it wasn't really a hut. It was more of a plantation house with rooms along the perimeter. There were no panes in the windows, just the open air and gentle breezes of Hawaii at dusk. The sunset was casting beautiful beams of pink-colored light as vapors of steam drifted down and into the rooms.

Layne, who had taken an earlier flight, was waiting for us at the entrance to the hut with leis she had made from assorted shells and flowers. She said she *loved* working in the kitchens, preparing meals, and harvesting the organic vegetable and herb gardens. She embraced each of us in a warm squeeze after giving us our lei. She smelled like patchouli, which quieted some of our misgivings. I, for one, felt a comfortable release. Whew! Finally, I had a feeling of home.

As we ascended the wooden steps to the lanai, laden with grocery bags and luggage, I tripped. I was the one carrying most of our spirits, and the *clang, clang, clang* reverberated throughout the entire living area. We all cringed at this unplanned announcement to the guardian angels. *Yikes!* This wasn't turning out well. Upon hearing the clinking bottles and our troop's subsequent laughter, Reverend Faith shouted loud and clear, "Silence! No talking or laughing!"

It took all my strength not to break down and crack up laughing. No talking or laughing? What the hell? This all seemed so ridiculous. That poor woman was probably realizing that when it came to our group, she was going to have her work cut out for her.

We crossed the threshold into the grand room, where we saw Uncle Ben's white rice clearly marking the sacred ceremonial circle. Literally, the empty Uncle Ben's cardboard box had been tossed haphazardly in the corner. Inside of the rice circle sat a stack of mats in assorted colors and Hawaiian prints. An altar of shells, sand, candles, shell necklaces, and huge floral arrangements had been constructed in front of the ten-foot-tall fireplace. The crude altar sat at the head of the circle facing north, which we later learned was somehow significant in allowing our angels to enter the room.

"It'll be hard to get our luggage up to our rooms," Torey said. "There's no space to roll our bags by." Indeed, we had a pathway of less than one foot wide between the rice circle and the walls. It would've taken an accomplished tightrope acrobat to get to the rooms without disturbing Uncle Ben. Suddenly, a wave of inner-child mischievousness washed over me, and I did a little Irish jig with my foot in and out of the circle. Kat and Torey gasped when Ziggy reached over with her perfectly manicured index finger to draw an S-shaped curve along the line of rice. Oh, our devious hearts were pounding. It crossed my mind that our angels might not ask the dolphins to come play with us unless we started behaving.

Unamused, Jeanne shook her head in motherly disapproval. I could tell she wanted to circle the wagons here and take some control over the situation. So she took it upon herself to assign each of us our rooms. Reaching over and grabbing Torey's luggage, she gently nudged her forward to share a room with Kat. Ziggy, Jeanne, and I took the other room.

Inside we found several single beds, one lamp, and a closet with a plug-in fan sitting on the floor. The walls were made of knotted pine, and the smell of incense lingered in the air. A simple acrylic painting of a naked woman with flowing blonde hair riding a white stallion hung on our wall. *Yup, this is a good sign that this is my room for sure.*

Tory and Kat's room had a small desk where we decided to stash our illegal libations. We were impressed with our little minibar and were about to pour our first drink when we heard my name called loudly. "Misha!" I jumped and scurried to the head of the stairs. The reverend, her hands still on her enormous hips, was standing below. "You have disrespected the angels by your antics with the sacred rice circle! They communicate with me and tell me everything. Now we will have to perform the purification all over again. Get your group down to the pool for your purifying salt scrubs posthaste! You are all obviously in need of them. Bring your towels. And don't *ever* touch the sacred rice circle again!"

Holy shit! We were left speechless, mouths agape and eyes bulging. How in the world did she see what we did to the rice circle? Ziggy hastily went over to the area she had desecrated and straightened it up. I wanted to do another jig with my toe, but I decided against it. "Come on, everyone," I said, breaking our shocked silence. "Posthaste!"

"Where are the bathrooms?" Kat wondered aloud.

Torey was in her room painting her toenails. She couldn't go quite yet. I told her we were going and to hurry it up. "Go ahead," she said. "I can meet you there."

We wandered down a path that looked like it would lead to the shore, listening to the birds' melodious songs as we went. We weren't really sure where we were supposed to go for this salt scrub, but still reeling from being in trouble, we didn't want to ask for directions. Jeanne told us to calm down, reminding us we hadn't really done anything wrong. We were grown women after all, and we were behaving like schoolgirls on the brink of being sent to the principal's office. Sheesh! We all laughed and agreed this was indeed going to be quite the experience. To comfort one another and soothe our frayed nerves, we linked arms as we continued our journey. Trying to stay positive, I tightened my hold with the arms linked through mine and began to skip. "We're off to see the wizard, the wonderful wizard of Oz!" I sang. "Because, because, because, because, becaaaaaaaaaause, because of the wonderful things he does!" With reckless abandon, everyone joined in the song. It didn't take us long to joyfully synchronize with one another.

When we reached the shore, we came upon another grass hut. Thinking this must be where the salt scrubs would take place, we entered. Inside there was a ceiling fan and several grass mats laid in a line on the ground. "Disrobe, and lie on a grass matt of your choosing," a man said. His deep voice startled us from within the hut. "You may cover yourselves with your towels."

When I made eye contact with the man who had spoken, I almost fainted! I knew him! He had been married to one of my sister's friends, and he was such a loser. I couldn't believe that this man would be the one performing our purification rituals! I made eye contact with him, and in that same moment, I could tell he recognized me too. He handed me a towel, noticing I had forgotten mine. Then smiled, and winked. *Gross*, I thought. He told us his name was Jay, but I knew differently. He said he was a master healer and massage therapist. If any of us would like a massage during our stay, we could schedule an appointment with him or his partner, Reverend Faith.

Obediently, we stripped, wrapped ourselves in our towels, and took our mats. On a nearby table sat half of a large coconut shell filled with salt and a big wooden pail brimming with ocean water. He began plastering salt on his hands and rubbing each of us down our arms and legs. Next he took the wooden pail and ladled ocean water onto us to rinse the salt away. Though the salt scrub had been scratchy, the warm ocean water, humid air, and soft music playing in the background had cast a peaceful spell over everyone— everyone but me. My mind was in a frenzy as I recalled everything I knew about this master healer. My thoughts were interrupted when Torey, toes perfectly painted, barged in, smiling happily.

"Sorry I'm late," she announced flippantly. "Oh! Uh … I forgot my towel." Jay introduced himself and handed her a towel, which she pinched by the corner and held as far away from herself as she could as though it might try to bite her. "Um … why is this towel wet? Is it clean?" she asked.

Jay assured her that the dampness was only pure ocean water from a sacred pond. Not quite convinced, Torey still held the towel between her two fingers while using her other hand to pick up her grass matt. She began shaking the mat to get the sand off, oblivious to the fact that she was spraying it all over me. I had already been rinsed and cleansed and was supposed to be meditating.

Jay went through the same ritual with Torey that he had just finished with us—rubbing salt scrub the length of her arms down to her fingertips and then starting at the knees and going down to each individual toe.

"Ouch!" Torey shrieked. "What are you doing? Oh my God, just look what you did to my toenail polish!"

Unable to contain ourselves, we all chuckled quietly, except for Torey, who was pissed. That concluded our purifying salt scrubs. We began collecting our clothes, eager to return to our rooms to unpack and make forbidden drinks when Jay pulled me aside. He caught me off-guard with a hug and then looked beseechingly into my eyes.

"Please," he whispered. "I beg of you. Please don't blow my cover."

I promised I wouldn't tell anyone—though I told everyone,

of course—and said his secret was safe with me. (After I told all my friends who this imposter was and revealed details about his real identity, we couldn't stop laughing about it.) We all had been betrayed and lied to by men in our lives, so it was unfortunate for him, that I knew his true story and he wasn't the person he was attempting to portray to us.

On the trek back to our rooms, I could sense that this place wasn't up to everyone's expectations, and I began to wonder what I had gotten my friends into. It was all becoming so … so absurd like a *Saturday Night Live* skit. Everything felt so extraterrestrial and weird. Torey was having an especially difficult time because of her need for perfection and control (not to mention she needed to paint her toenails bubblegum pink all over again.)

Before reaching our rooms, we stopped at the outdoor community showers to wash off the salt scrub fiasco. They were quaint and open, and they sprayed fresh cool water rinsing our bodies. Kat and Jeanne were singing a song as loudly as their lungs would let them when we heard someone yelling over them, "*Be quiet!* Stop that singing! I am right here next to you, meditating and napping."

Of course, it was our favorite reverend. My God, this woman was a real piece of work. I had been hoping our angels had come together, encouraging us to sing and laugh and move beyond the craziness of our first few hours here. Despite everything, I was still holding on to the hope of meeting my angels. I knew I had some. Nobody could have a life as wonderful and as blessed as mine without having at least a few. I'd been gifted with the most beautiful, amazing, and loving friends who had trusted me enough to join me on this wild ride on the wings of angels and the fins of dolphins. Oh, how I prayed things would take a turn for the better soon.

4

When we unpacked, we discovered that between the five of us, we had more than twenty-five pairs of sandals, flip-flops, tennis shoes, and flats! *Leave it to a handful of women*, I mused. Torey had the most, making her the winner, but her feet were smaller than the rest of ours, so we couldn't share most of our shoes with her. As Kat tried on a pair of Jeanne's strappy sandals, she shared her upbeat take on this whole trip so far. She thought Reverend Faith or "the Rev," as Kat nicknamed her, was a hoot! Ziggy was absolutely tickled by the creation of the nickname. "What fun we're all going to have!" she exclaimed, full of giggles.

While we were unpacking, I kept hearing a soft mewling sound. It was so tiny and faint that I had to cock my head numerous times. "Shhhhh," I hushed Ziggy and Jeanne, who were chatting away by the chest of alcohol. We listened for a moment but heard nothing. As soon as we returned to unpacking, I heard it again. "Listen!" I repeated.

It was quiet for a few moments, but then there it was again, a soft sound coming from the closet.

"Misha, you're crazy," Jeanne said as I pressed my ear to the closet door.

"I don't hear anything," Ziggy agreed.

"Nope," I protested. "For sure I hear something." When I quietly opened the closet, the sound became more distinct. A musty odor wafted from the darkness. Yuck. The smell was strong. As I moved a few pillows, I heard it again. "I think it's a kitten. Quick! Come over here and listen."

Everyone poked their head into the closet and finally heard what I'd been hearing. It sounded like it was coming from the top shelf. I pulled over a chair to stand on so that I could reach. As I stood up and peered over the top, we heard it again.

"Don't just reach up there!" Torey whispered worriedly as I blindly felt around the top shelf. "It could be something with rabies or a rat or something worse. Who knows?"

That made me laugh. Torey had developed a major rat phobia after her brother chased her around the block with a dead rat when she was a little girl. I was pretty sure this was a kitten, not a rat. When my eyes adjusted to the darkness of the closet, I found a skinny, bedraggled little kitten with tiny, wide-open eyes and a sweet little face huddled in the farthest back corner. It couldn't have been more than five weeks old. I reached back and scooped it into my palm, it felt like I was holding a bundle of toothpicks covered in fur. It started purring immediately. I could feel every little bone in its scrawny body. Carefully, I stepped down from the chair and presented it to its new mommies. I flipped it over. "Congratulations, we have a girl!"

Ziggy, who had already befriended one of the cooks, said, "Let's take her down to the kitchen and see if anyone has any idea where she came from. We can get some goat's milk for her too."

We agreed as I pulled a blanket off the shelf. I was about

to wrap our little kitten in it when Jeanne noticed brown stains all over it. "What is that? Poop?" she asked in disgust. We took turns scrutinizing and sniffing it. It wasn't cat poop according to my expert nose.

"Nope," I said. "Smells like human feces to me." After three children, dozens of cats, and a few years working for a proctologist, my trained nose could distinguish human excrement.

Ziggy and I decided to take the dirty blanket and our little furry kitten down past the rice circle and out into the starry night to look for goat's milk and some answers. We succeeded with the goat's milk and learned from the cook that the river had overflowed a month ago. She told us that a litter of kittens had been living under our hut, but everyone assumed the mother and kittens had been swept away by the flood. How this little one made it was beyond anyone's imagination. As for the soiled blanket, the cook explained that the group of guests prior to us had been part of a homosexual health and colonics retreat. Ziggy asked me what *colonics* meant, but after I explained, she thought it best not to tell anyone else. I agreed, but it was too good of a story not to tell Jeanne. She and I told each other everything!

Over the next several days, I took that kitten with me everywhere in my pocket or beach bag and fed her goat's milk and brown rice. After a few days, she began to thrive. She slept with me every night, curled around my neck like a little snail. One day as gently as possible, we gave her a warm bath using some natural soap provided by one of the cooks. She was so tiny when she was wet! Even as we bathed her, she wasn't scared and never tried to scratch us. Actually, she purred the whole time as we loved her and soothed her with baby talk. We named her Chewy because she was as small as a gummy bear and loved chewing on my hair. Between the kitchen staff, my friends, and me, we took care of sweet Chewy with much love and devotion.

Dinner was announced throughout the camp by the sound of a deep, resonating gong that people could hear throughout the entire camp. After we downed the remainder of our alcoholic beverages in a hurry, we hustled to put our name tags around our necks. Once there, surveying the food tables, I became totally ecstatic about what was presented to us, beautifully displayed with lush leaves and an array of colorful tropical flowers. Everything was organic and fresh. Healthy, raw veggies and tropical fruit salads lined the buffet table along with mahi-mahi that had been caught in the bay earlier that day, enhanced by a delicious tartar sauce made from homemade pickles, mayonnaise, fresh dill, and lemon. There were also baskets of freshly baked breads, brown rice, quinoa, beans, dates, figs, avocados, and tamari. I salivated over the fresh herb dips made with goat cheese and the two pureed sauces—one made with tomatoes and onions, the other with papaya, pineapple chutney, lemon, and lime juice.

Ziggy and Jeanne missed carbs big time. Ziggy realized she was detoxing, while Torey thought the food was boring. "I, for one, do *not* like these bland foods," Torey said, dropping her fork on her plate in disgust. "This is not what we paid for."

Steadfast in her Pollyannaish outlook on life, Kat said she truly enjoyed eating such a variety of healthy foods. I loved the whole spread. It was pretty much what I was accustomed to feeding my family, just a bit more rigid. I prayed that my friends would all be satisfied by the sugar in our treasure chest of alcohol later. Even if they didn't like the food, at least they liked the friendly cooking staff. They seemed to love us too, and they wanted to be our friends' right out of the gate.

After dinner we went right into the welcoming ceremony,

which was located inside of our hut's circle of rice. The rich fragrance of plumeria and vanilla cedar incense filled the air. White candles flickered gently in the evening breezes that trickled through the windows. We lined up around the sacred rice circle and looked to Reverend Faith, who was standing inside of the circle with an air of self-importance, as we patiently stood, waiting for further instruction. Wearing a flowing red Kaftan made of chiffon, she actually looked quite beautiful in her own way. She instructed us to enter the sacred circle in a single-file line, hugging and blessing each of us as we passed through. She whispered in our ears a truth to each of us as well—a truth she believed we needed to be aware of. Layne walking with confidence leaned in to hear "You are an old soul, reawakening all that you have forgotten" Kat heard the words, "You are angry and go unnoticed. You feel that you are not appreciated." Ziggy heard, "You are a lost soul. You must find your path and hold fast." Torey heard, "You must learn to let go." Jeanne heard, "Beware the path on which you are headed. Only you have the answers you are seeking. You must face them head-on." And I heard, "Only you can help your group come together as one, and you had better start right away. You need this lesson most of all."

We took our seats inside the circle. Reverend Faith began by sharing a bit about herself and her credentials. She claimed to have lived in a Tibetan monastery for seven years with a group of monks who had taken vows of silence. I couldn't fathom such a life. You would have to cut out my tongue in order for me to follow such rules. She never explained what compelled her to go to Tibet. Later, we heard rumors that she had volunteered to go there for seven years as some kind of redemption for evil things she had done in her past lifetimes. Regardless, I was surprised to find myself impressed by her knowledge of the history regarding meditation and prayer.

"Our native elders have taught us that before people

can be healed or heal others, they must be cleansed of any bad feelings, negative thoughts, angry spirits, and negative energy—cleansed both physically and spiritually," she explained in her booming voice. "This helps the healing to come through in a clear way without being distorted or sidetracked by negative energy in either the healer or the client. The elders say that all ceremonies, tribal or private, must be entered into with a good heart so that we can pray, sing, and walk in a sacred manner and be helped by the spirits to enter the sacred realms. Native people throughout the world use herbs to accomplish this. One common ceremony is to burn certain herbs, take the smoke into one's hands, and brush it over the body. This is commonly called smudging, and we will perform a version of this cleansing ritual today with the use of sage."

Next the reverend lit a bundle of sage on fire and began fanning the resulting smoke in our direction. We were then *smudged* with the wand of burning sage, and we were also instructed to open our arms wide and to breathe deeply. We had to pull the sage smoke into our heart chakras. Wow, that smoke was strong! When Torey started choking and coughing dramatically, Reverend Faith's response was to wave more smoke toward her. I was familiar with the practice, but I didn't know how much my friends knew about it. Noticing Torey's red, swollen eyes, I knew she certainly wasn't impressed. *Great*, I thought. *Watch her be allergic to sage. Just our luck.* I tried to keep Chewy, who was snuggled in my pocket, from inhaling the smoke billowing around us. Reverend Faith must have thought we really needed to cleanse away years of sin.

We ended the ceremony holding hands and sending positive energy from our hearts to the dolphins. We invited our angels to be with us and to reveal themselves in the week ahead. The Rev told us to be aware and to seek our angels in everything we saw and experienced throughout the rest of our time at the retreat. She taught us how to turn our bodies into tuning forks for higher consciousness. I was absolutely baffled by the change in her demeanor and was in awe of her suddenly eloquent speech. She taught us breathing techniques to cleanse our chakras and open our hearts to the gifts that would assuredly be blessed upon us in the ensuing days. After she closed the ceremony with a sweet prayer, we bowed to the altar of candles, flowers, and shells as we exited. It reminded Kat and me of the days when we passed and knelt before Catholic altars, taking symbolic wine and wafers.

We left quietly with strict instructions that there was to be no talking for the next hour. Amazingly, we all abided. I'm a talker, and this was one of the hardest things I have ever done in my life. I have what people sometimes referred to as "monkey mind," and it is so difficult for it to be still and quiet. Over the years I have come to realize that I most definitely have ADD. I loved hot Bikram Yoga because it was the only discipline I could find to quiet my mind. I was so in the moment with each challenging pose and the intense heat that the only thing my waggling monkey mind had room to focus on was how to survive each second. I was also able to discipline my focus when riding my horse Sai Moon. Every class I entered during competition, as I focused on becoming one with him, it would feel like he was an extension of me. All I had to do was think *trot*, *canter*, or *walk*, and he knew what to do. Once I described this connection to my trainer, who told me that if a horse can feel a fly land on his body, he certainly can feel his rider's next command. As subtle as the cues were, I would simply think a command in my mind, and without much thought or deliberate effort, my body would shift its weight, step into a stirrup as Sai Moon would begin shifting into our next transition.

Knowing how difficult being silent would be for me as soon as the task was announced, Jeanne immediately came over to me with a stern look in her gorgeous gold-flecked eyes that lovingly said, "Shut up." In her motherly way, she guided me to bed, kissed her fingertips, pressed them to my forehead, pulled my blanket over my head, and then slid Chewy in next to me. She knew that tucking me into bed would be the only way to help me keep silent for the next hour. Thinking about Reverend Faith's experience with the silent Tibetan monks inspired me to force myself to accomplish this little exercise. I succeeded.

5

The island's southeast shore is popular for its frequent sea turtle sightings, which we were fortunate enough to experience on our fourth morning at the resort. They came into view as the moon was lost behind a thin, opalescent layer of clouds and the sunrise was just beginning to paint the sky with faint, glowing pinks and oranges. To witness the sinking moon and watch the rising sun simultaneously was a once in a lifetime extraordinary experience for us all.

This morning marked our first free day at the beach since our arrival—thank God. We needed a real tropical experience, relaxing and enjoying the piña coladas and mai tais hidden in our water bottles. I even ventured to ask the chef with the long dreadlocks if he knew where I could score some good weed. Apparently, he was the right person to ask because he had some right there in his pocket. He gave it to me for free, but he said the next batch would cost fifty bucks. Let this new day begin!

We asked around to learn which beach the locals preferred. To get to it, we had to hike over a rough terrain of black lava rock that made it more difficult to navigate in flip-flops. I took mine off, and so did Kat, Jeanne, and Ziggy. Torey left hers on, saying that she had very sensitive feet.

As we traipsed along, the rocky trail gradually turned into the finest black sand I had ever seen or felt. I bent over to pick up a handful and let it trickle through my fingers like water. Silver and white crystalline grains of sand were mixed in with the black, and they glistened in the sunlight as they fell from my hand. It was too beautiful for words. Or maybe the pot I'd just smoked was enhancing the effect. Either way, I was enthralled and excited to begin another adventure with my team of friends.

Layne couldn't come with us, but she had packed us an amazing lunch—mixed nuts in tamari, a few cucumbers, raw cheeses, avocados, tahini sauce sandwiches on a delicious homemade bread, pineapple slices, mango slices, and of course, our cooler filled with ice and alcohol. However, lugging it all the way to the beach was turning out to be quite exhausting.

"Are you sure this is the right path?" Torey asked, wiping beads of sweat from her brow. "We've been walking a long time."

"Yup," Jeanne said. "This is it. We're almost there."

Kat agreed. My sense of direction was nonexistent, so I just followed along, smiling and feeling good about my thin, liposuctioned thighs. I couldn't wait to swim in the ocean. As we came over the crest of the last hill, we saw the most beautiful black sand beach we had ever seen! Actually, none of us had ever seen a black sand beach before, but nonetheless, it was breathtaking. On our island there were four unique types of beaches—black sand, green sand, white sand, and salt and pepper. At some point, we planned to seize our next opportunity to visit a green sand beach where the sand was created from olivine crystals. As we stood there, triumphantly taking in the beauty from the top of the last hill of our trek, the realization came to us slowly, and when it finally dawned on us, the words were already leaving Torey's lips. "It's a nudist beach!" she cried in horror.

Sheepishly making our way down to the beach, we couldn't help but gawk at the men walking along the shore and the beautiful women sunbathing and swimming.

"Uh-uh, no way," Ziggy mumbled. "I am *not* taking my suit off!"

"Well, you don't have to if you don't want to," I said. "Look. A few people have left their bottoms on."

The climb down the top of the cliff was a bit treacherous, and Torey, who still refused to take off her flip-flops, kept slipping. I reached the bottom first and told everyone to toss their beach bags and sandals down to me so they could use their hands to help them with the last bit of the descent. I finally convinced Torey to throw me her damn sandals, which had slippery leather soles. She was the last one to land safely.

It was a glorious day! The surf was perfect, and the whole ocean glistened in the sunlight. It looked like someone had tossed glitter all over the ground. I found a spot on the shore to lay down my towel. Jeanne spread her towel next to mine, while Kat, Ziggy, and Torey posted up directly behind us.

I was the first to strip. My husband and I had owned a hot tub for years and never went in with suits on, so being nude wasn't a novelty to me. Besides, I felt comfortable in my own skin, and worked in an environment where clothes off was a familiar sight. Jeanne was having her period, so she couldn't take her bottoms off. We wondered aloud if she was going to attract sharks and decided none of us would swim with her. Ziggy was a little hesitant about taking her suit off, and since this was Torey's first trip to a tropical island, the nude beach was initially way out of her comfort zone. She loosened up after a few mai tais though, embracing a newfound feeling of freedom. She was shedding the ropes that had tied her down for her entire life.

I turned over on my belly to say something to Kat, but instead got an unexpected eyeful of her wide-open legs, revealing her completely shaved beaver! "Holy shit!" I exclaimed, taken aback. "Look at Kat's ... well, her vagina! You can see everything!" Having never seen a Brazilian wax before, I was surprised and transfixed. She must have been the first of us to shave everywhere, or so I assumed. Jeanne, Ziggy, and Torey admitted that they regularly shaved their bikini lines, but not the whole mons pubis area. We had to laugh and admitted it was kind of sexy. I had let my husband shave me once down there as a fun thing to do, but it was so itchy growing back that we never did it again. I only had to shave my legs and armpits once in a while, but Jeanne said she had to shave every day! I reached over and rubbed her leg. It felt rough like my husband's five o'clock shadow. It seemed like we were learning something new about one another and ourselves every day.

Each day something new seemed to tug at our comfort zones. Together as a whole, we helped reduce the uncomfortable tugging whenever one of the others felt it. I could see that being pushed out of our comfort zones ultimately made us feel more at ease with ourselves—with who we were and who we wanted to become. We were all in our early thirties and forties, and we all thought we already knew who we were and what we wanted out of life. But in retrospect, we were still growing our roots, seeking sunshine, and trying to blossom. We didn't realize it consciously, but we were searching for what moonlight brings to a wandering soul lost in the darkness of the night. Sun, moonbeams, dolphins, and angels were exactly what we five women needed at that stage of our lives. We yearned for that perfect equilibrium of grace and happiness in our hectic lives. The laughter, stories, and love shared that day could fill a book.

I was always fascinated with the ideas of moon phases or menstrual cycles throughout history. Some cultures sequestered women during their moon phases. I thought that was a *great* idea! We could get away from men and children and our busy, day-to-day routines. Set us free, and maybe then we wouldn't be such bitches. When young women would begin menstruation, they would join the other menstruating women, who could in turn teach them the ancient lessons that need to be passed on from generation to generation, from woman to woman.

Out of the corner of my eye, I noticed Jeanne putting on her wetsuit. She and I had always had a playfully competitive relationship, always trying to one-up each other. Sometimes we got ourselves into pickles, but we always came through laughing. When I saw her donning her wetsuit, I was confused. "Huh?" I said. "It's Hawaii! You don't need a wetsuit!"

"Well, you know I'm a diver," she said. "I'm used to always wearing it. Plus it's buoyant, and it'll make me feel safe when I swim out there past those farthest waves!" She winked at me mischievously.

"No, Jeanne, don't do that," I begged. "Please! I can't take the stress. Besides, how much have you had to drink? Are you sure you're really safe to swim right now?"

"I'm fine. I feel great."

She just arched an eyebrow and shot me that familiar, challenging look that always got us into trouble. "Come with me," she dared.

Well, I did have my Styrofoam noodle horse, so I felt pretty confident that I could go with her. We took off running into the crystal clear ocean with Kat and Ziggy on our heels. They stayed back, riding the waves and playing in the surf as Jeanne and I ventured out to deeper waters. When we could swim no farther, Jeanne grabbed onto my noodle, and we floated. From way out beyond the surf, I watched my sweet, beautiful, all-embracing friends with so much gratitude and awe. We were a team.

Torey kept an eye on all of us from her towel on the sandy black shore. I waved and sent heartfelt words of song to her, my dear friend since we were five years old.

"Jeanne, let's swim back," I said. "Torey's never swam in the ocean before, and I think she'd like to join us."

"*What?*" Jeanne exclaimed in alarm. But it wasn't my comment that astounded her. At that moment, Torey was wading into the surf to join Kat and Zig, and she was still wearing her Versace sunglasses and the leather Gucci flip-flops that matched her swimsuit.

"Come on out, Tor. The water is perfect," Kat yelled.

"You're gonna love it!" Ziggy chimed.

"No! No! Take off your sandals!" Jeanne screamed, but we were too far out for Torey to hear us. I sensed where Jeanne was coming from. Torey didn't have a clue about ocean currents or surf.

"Torey, take *off* your sunglasses and sandals!" I shouted.

Jeanne and I finally caught the attention of Kat and Ziggy, who suddenly realized what was happening. Kat told Torey to back up, and Ziggy told her to take off her expensive sunglasses. I started swimming toward the shore as fast as I could, bobbing throughout the waves and riding a few with Jeanne, who was definitely doing better with the help of that wet suit. But Torey was too enthralled with the experience to listen to any of us. "Oh, this water is so warm and so beautiful," she babbled as she waded out. "It's better than bathwater! What? Don't worry! I don't want to get my hair wet or ruin my makeup. I won't come out that far—"

"*Watch out!*" the four of us cried in unison.

But we were too late. A large wave washed over Torey,

sending her ass over teakettle under the water. She came up, spluttering, scared, and completely discombobulated. We swam to help and tried to calm her down. She couldn't believe how salty the water was. Her eyes were stinging, and she'd lost her sandals and her $300 sunglasses! We searched and searched, but we found only one sandal that had washed ashore. Since none of us had goggles, we couldn't open our eyes underwater for very long. Torey offered a couple of young kids a reward if they found her sunglasses—ten bucks per kid to start with. Each of us offered to add another ten dollars, but Torey's designer sunglasses with the prescription lenses were never found.

"Well, consider it a gift to the dolphins we'll be swimming with soon," I whispered encouragingly to Torey as I put my arm around her shoulders. When it was time to leave, Torey didn't like the idea of walking all the way back without her sandals. Since I often walked barefoot, my feet were tough and calloused, so I gave Torey my plastic flip-flops. Even though they were the wrong color for her swimsuit and four sizes too big for her tiny feet, she was a little trooper. As she flip-flopped along without a word of complaint, we were all impressed. We knew how hard it was for her to accept the loss of her sunglasses and sandals. At least her toenail polish, which she had meticulously fixed after Jay had ruined it with his salt scrub, looked perfect.

After our nude beach adventure, we hopped into our van to head back to the retreat. Along the way we picked up a cute hitchhiker, smoked some of his hash, and drank the container of piña coladas we had left in the car. We arrived at home base inebriated and singing at the tops of our lungs. The sun was setting, casting a peaceful solitude over us as we showered and put on our name tags. Somehow, we had reached a sublime, unspoken feeling that said, "Forget about makeup. Forget about hair. Let's just go as we are." We flowed seamlessly into this mentality and space of just letting ourselves *be*. That was pretty crazy for a bunch of women who always used beauty aids to look beautiful and perfect.

After our day at the beach, we were famished. For the first time, everybody loved the night's meal. Dinner was wild-caught, local fish that had been simmered in smooth papaya-mango sauce. We loved the sauce that was on the fish and soaked our brown rice and homemade bread in it. Dessert was a frozen pineapple, lime, and spearmint compote layered in honey from a local honeybee plantation. We smothered it in creamy goat's milk, agreeing we were in heaven. (Or maybe we were being influenced by the Maui Wowie we had smoked earlier.) Whatever the reason, we had found a bliss I didn't want any of us to lose.

Sadly, that night our sacred ceremony turned into a total nightmare.

6

There I was, imagining we all had found bliss with our tan and smiling faces without any makeup, our hair au naturel, and our bellies full. Every evening's rice circle started with a prayer in which we all held hands and bowing our heads, as if in prayer. We would then take a few steps back to sit on the mats that were placed around the inside of the circle. Reverend Faith used two or sometimes three mats stacked on top of one another. She was too big and not limber enough to sit as we did.

This evening she remained standing as the rest of us took to our mattresses for the evening's lesson. She began speaking about Christianity, Buddhism, and other religions. "I feel there is discord among us!" she suddenly shouted—a tone we were becoming accustomed to. "I would like for everyone to let go of distrust, angst, anger, jealousy, and animosity toward one another. Then share with the group what is in your heart. Be honest! Come forth!"

Keeping my head bowed, I didn't dare look into my friends' eyes, terrified of the honesty that might bubble from one of our hearts in the form of a giggle. We had learned early on not to make eye contact with one another during these ceremonies. Eye contact could lead to an eye roll, which could lead to stifled giggles, which would inevitably set us all off into fits of laughter. Refraining from making eye contact also allowed us to dive deeply into our own sacred spaces with our private thoughts.

Reverend Faith said something about gratefulness, prayer, meditation, and breathing exercises, but still, no one stepped up. We were waiting in anticipation of someone taking the stage when the Rev herself came forward. "My heart be still!" she cried, melodramatically clasping a hand to her chest. I thought for sure she was going to lay into each of us for the alcohol, marijuana, laughter after lights-out, and everything else we were doing to disgust our angels and sully ourselves before the sacred dolphins. When she exhaled deeply, we followed suit. *Breathe in, breathe out. Let it all go.* But then she began bellowing like a beached whale, "I am furious with my partner! He has stolen my trust and the money from this retreat!"

This had gone from bad to worse. I couldn't help wonder what on earth my friends were thinking in that moment. I certainly didn't know what to think. Maybe we should have followed Jeanne's lead earlier when she'd downed a bottle of wine before attending the ceremony. Next thing you know, Jay (who really wasn't Jay) stepped into the circle and stood face-to-face with the Rev. "You are the devil!" he cried. "You are the one who screwed *me* over! You stole *my* money!"

Jerry Springer didn't have a show at the time, but if he had, this scene would have really been something to witness. What a fight! And how disgusting and disappointing to realize that Jay and Faith might have been more than just business partners. This animosity and argument in front of everyone was ludicrous. Truthfully, I couldn't imagine Jay in a relationship with Reverend Faith, possibly because of what

I knew about the Jay who'd been married to my sister's friend, but my friends all claimed it was obvious.

Next the fight escalated into something totally surreal with bad energy flying everywhere. I couldn't even make out what they were shouting at each other anymore. I buried my head between my arms and then glanced at Jeanne, but we quickly broke our eye contact so we wouldn't break into laughter although this, wasn't a laughing matter. Then Layne, who was always steadfast and honorable in her quest for peace, stepped forward into the circle. Raising her arms, she spoke words of wisdom about not letting ourselves be burdened with other people's issues. She started, "We must see everything as a lesson to overcome any antagonism toward others as this will only lead to further hardships within ourselves. Each must learn acceptance. Don't allow yourself to take on others problems and issues. They have nothing to do with who you are. This belongs to them. This is their own disharmony within themselves." Quieting our distressed spirits, she brought us back into harmony with all that was good. We all lowered our heads and wept. By drawing us into our heart chakras, Layne inspired us to weep with love and joy as she guided us back to the path of releasing our doubts, fears, and frustrations. Her wisdom released us from the anger and disappointment we had accumulated over the past few days and perhaps over our lifetimes.

We were released early from that night's ceremony. As we left the circle, nobody stepped on the pillows and Uncle Ben's rice didn't lose a single grain. We solemnly breathed in the full moon as we continued to process Layne's words. Was what we witnessed and experienced that evening a giant step toward who we were becoming?

Emotionally exhausted, we entered our rooms, blew fingertip kisses to one another, and got ready for bed. Ziggy and Jeanne went out to the open air bathrooms to wash their faces and brush their teeth. After retrieving Chewy from her bed in the kitchen, I somberly trudged up to our room, but I couldn't sleep. Unable to turn off my monkey mind, I turned on my nightlight and read until nearly dawn. I realized how much I needed Craig, and missed him so deeply that I prayed to my guardian angel for some kind of safety net to catch me, lending me to a cocoon of sleep and dreams. I felt like I was falling into an empty void, and I kept searching for my angel, hoping desperately that we would find each other sooner rather than later. Craig has always been close to comfort me during any disharmony or discord when tempers flare around me. I had lived in a family where my parents were continuously fighting and yelling about money issues, and in hindsight. After money issues, I was having difficulty facing those childhood feelings that had erupted, rearing their ugly heads. Finally, I dozed off imagining I was riding SaiMoon in the ocean waves.

7

O ur next morning began with the obnoxious breakfast gong, which seemed to sound the moment I had finally fallen asleep. Ziggy prodded me awake, telling me to "get shakin' because breakfast is awaitin'!"

"Come on," Jeanne said. "I'll make us a couple of Bloody Marys to get us going before we head out."

"It's a little early for Bloody Marys. Maybe we should convince everyone to take a day off alcohol and drink the delicious lemonade or papaya juice or fresh pineapple juices," I said, reluctantly rolling out of bed. "But I could use some tea."

"Okay, but you'll change your mind after we eat breakfast."

At breakfast Jeanne and Kat had finally gotten used to the no-coffee rule and went directly for the assorted teas and honey. We were also getting accustomed to the goat's milk. Ziggy and I always had the oatmeal with goat milk for breakfast. I liked to doctor mine up with seeds, walnuts, bananas, coconut flakes, and honey. It tasted like ambrosia, and I was looking forward to it every morning. I had never been a huge fan of fruit, but fresh fruit was everywhere. I considered myself more of a veggie person than a fruity person, although at times I suppose I was a little *fruity*.

Today was another free day, and we decided to spend it at the retreat's pool. With our sights set high for the day, we were anxious to compare notes about last night's craziness between Reverend Faith and Jay. The pool was modest in size but quaint with its wooden lattice fencing. Bougainvillea draped itself over the fencing, and the fragrance of plumeria wafted in the breeze. I picked a large bouquet of flowers and tossed them into the saltwater pool so we could swim among them all day. Next to the pool was a gorgeous cedar hot tub surrounded by flowers and vines. We had the pool all to ourselves until a few of the retreat staff joined us. Together, we drank cocktails (made from our illicit stash and the assorted juices we had smuggled out of the cafeteria that morning). I guess so much for a "no alcohol day" I mused to myself. After smoking a doobie provided by our friend with the dreadlocks, we drifted off to nowhere land, holding our sides, which ached with laughter.

One of the chefs who was a darling lesbian had taken a liking to our Ziggy. In an attempt to impress Ziggy, she made all of us delicious, whole grain sandwiches with avocados, lettuce, tomatoes, olives, and homemade mustard. All of us were moaning in ecstasy because they were so good. Her special cookies were over-the-top delicious, and she had brought fresh coconut pineapple juice that was sublime. Realizing this woman had a little crush on her, Ziggy became enamored with the attention. She seemed to really enjoy this woman's wavering touch as she rubbed oils onto Ziggy's body at a secluded spot near the pool. But we could also tell that Ziggy was nervous, because she kept coming back to us for more cocktails.

After a few hours, Jeanne and I returned to the room

to mix a few more drinks since Ziggy had been sucking down our first batch at an impressive rate. We were mixing away, chatting, laughing, and playing with Chewy when Kat entered. She had scheduled a massage with Jay at noon, but when he failed to show up, she went looking for him. Finally, she ran into Layne, who informed her that Jay was no longer a part of the retreat staff. We couldn't wait to bring this juicy bit of news back to the pool.

We drank and gossiped all day, except for Ziggy, who sequestered herself away from the group with the darling lesbian chef. When the sun began to settle beyond the horizon, it was time to return to our rooms. With her loving understanding of the whole situation, Jeanne gently tried to pry Ziggy away from her new paramour. She put her arm around Ziggy's shoulders and said, "C'mon, sweetie, just walk. One foot in front of the other—that's right." When Ziggy would spin off in another direction, Jeanne would grab her up again and assist her with walking. At one point she even had to get behind Ziggy and use her own legs to push our drunken friend forward in a marionette-like march. It was quite the comedy act, but we could all empathize. We had all been there many times before. I certainly knew I had. Ziggy was the baby of our little group, and no one passed judgment on her. She learned an important lesson that night. One should never mix different types of alcohol.

As soon as we reached our room, Ziggy plopped onto her bed and groaned. Very aware of what was coming, Jeanne and I exchanged glances and then took off in a frenzied search for something Ziggy could puke into. Jeanne found a wicker wastebasket just in the nick of time. "I just don't understand," Ziggy said, pulling her head out of the basket. "I think it may have been the rum. No, wait. Maybe the vodka … or the gin. Hold it, hold it. For sure it was the tequila shots. Oh yeah, had to be the tequila. I *always* get sick when I drink tequila." (Yeah, right. We had another great laugh after that comment!)

When the dinner gong sounded, Ziggy thought that skipping dinner would be a good idea. I laughed and agreed as I wiped her brow with a cool, wet washcloth. With her basket and a bottle of water close by, we left her to sleep it off.

Ziggy also missed our prayer circle that evening, which ended with a powerful, tantric exercise. Layne gave each of us a candle that represented our personal angels. She explained that tantric meditation can be practiced alone or by couples, but it is generally practiced in a group setting since this allows for a greater buildup of synergistic tantric energy.

"Within each of us—specifically in the region of the tailbone—a bundle of energy is waiting to unfold and transform us," Layne explained. "The idea behind tantra meditation is to allow this energy to ascend through the various centers of power—the tantra chakras—to the crown chakra. It must be stressed that this is primeval energy in its unformed state. Though it can facilitate powerful personal growth, it can also do harm if it's allowed to flow without proper guidance. In other words, tantra meditation should not be practiced without first experiencing it with the supervision and instruction of an experienced tantra master. Under the right conditions, it can be a life-changing experience. A tantra master can teach us to harness and utilize the energy generated during such a meditation session to vastly improve our sex lives, interpersonal relationships, and our ability to deal with the various stresses and challenges of modern life. Do not seek shortcuts to finding and using the power of tantra meditation. It is of the utmost importance to have a tantra teacher to guide you every step of the way, to show you how to overflow with divine power, confidence, and an unbelievable joy of life."

When it was time to begin our tantra exercise, we entered

the sacred circle, lit our angel candles, said our blessings, and opened our hearts to everything good, great, and beyond wonderful. It was tattooed onto our being, an experience no words could describe. A soft breeze rustled the leaves outside the hut. The birds were sleeping, so a soft silence filled the evening, and the moon and stars cast a shiny, silver light into the hut.

We were instructed to choose partners and sit cross-legged across from one another in a process that would take two hours. Without words, Layne and I sat down facing each other. We stared into each other's eyes without talking, just sitting with our hands resting palms up on our thighs. We were told to just be in the moment with our partners, staring forward and communicating through our eyes, watching each other's breath, synchronizing our inhalations and exhalations.

After getting past the lower back pain, we learned to breathe fully into our own being and the being sitting across from us. Soon we were talking with our hearts, our eyes filled with tears. As our tears silently dispelled any misgivings or negative thoughts, we experienced a pure, intense, electrical touching of souls that radiated in our cores. It was wonderful.

I knew that Layne and I might never have an experience like the one we'd had that evening. She and I had entered a secret space between our breasts, connecting our heart chakras, opening a divine road into one another's unconscious minds. I felt light as air. I never wanted to forget this feeling. I planted the memory of the experience firmly in my heart chakra to take with me throughout my life.

When the soft harp music signaling the end of our rice circle ceremony came on, I wasn't ready to leave. I was still thirsty for something, but I didn't know what – just something else, something more. Was this what we were all searching so desperately for?

The moon was bright that night, and after the end of

the ceremony, we decided to relax together on the lanai surrounding our hut. We gazed up at the skies freckled with constellations from north to south, east to west. I pointed out the Milky Way and Orion above us, both of which lit the sky with their brilliance. Torey, Kat, Jeanne, and I all found the Big Dipper at the same exact moment. Suddenly feeling very connected, we looked at one another, hugged, and touched cheeks, full of love and gratitude for our friendship. We sent blessings to poor Ziggy, laughing and hoping she was doing okay. Jeanne had gone to check on her earlier and found her sleeping soundly, her sweet little hands folded under her cheek. We had put together a plate of food for her from dinner, so she could have something to eat once she woke from her drunken stupor. Just then, Ziggy suddenly appeared beside us on the lanai. "Hey, here I am! Did I miss anything?"

"Yeah," Kat said. "We were just missing you and talking about you, and now here you are!"

"This is such a strange vacation, you guys," Ziggy said.

"And it just keeps getting stranger," I replied with a laugh.

"I just love all of you so much," Torey whispered.

"You guys are manifesting this whole thing," Jeanne said, lighting up a cigarette.

Extremely addicted to nicotine, Jeanne usually took a cigarette break after our nightly ceremony. She started out taking her cigarette breaks alone, but as each evening passed, someone else joined her. Soon Kat, Torey, and Ziggy were smoking with her every night. One evening I found all of them smoking together on the lanai. "Oh my God, I never knew you *all* smoked like this!" I had cried. Then I asked them to give me a cigarette. None of them would. They said, "Absolutely not," and they meant it. I never knew what to make of their adamant refusal—except to assume that they all loved me too much to see me holding a cigarette, let alone actually smoking one. Perhaps they all knew I had an addictive personality. Whatever their reason, I stopped asking, imagining my friends standing in full armor, protecting me.

Together again, the five of us stood under the canopy of the Milky Way, drinking lemon tea, contemplating our dreams, laughing again and again, finding once more that elusive bit of bliss we had come here to experience. Kat said something that had us laughing so hard our cheeks hurt, and before long, we were holding our stomachs gasping for breath. In the distance, sexy jazz music was playing softly, and Torey started dancing and doing a striptease. It was the most beautiful dance, and we all agreed it could compete with the routines of the best professional dancers. However, our laughter and Torey's dance were abruptly interrupted by a loud shriek coming from the direction of Reverend Faith's room. I jumped at the sound.

"Oh my God, that sounded like the Rev," Kat said.

"I'm gonna go find out if she's okay," I said. The path to her room was dark, and I didn't have a candle or flashlight, so I had to step cautiously in the darkness. But once my eyes adjusted, I saw her enormous form outside of the entrance to her hut. "Was that you who yelled?" I whispered. I could tell that I had startled her. "Are you okay?"

I was shocked to see she was smoking a cigarette! Embarrassed, she tried to conceal it at her side. I felt uncomfortable for busting her and didn't comment on the cigarette. It was obvious she didn't want me to see it.

"I feel isolated and left out just as I always felt in junior high and high school," she replied quietly and without emotion. I had to lean in close to hear her words, and in the moonlight I noticed tears forming in her eyes. "Nobody liked me. I was bullied relentlessly, and all the popular girls teased me mercilessly. I am resentful of all that you and your friends share, and I realize I have never had and never will have that closeness or bond with another woman. My own mother thought I was a loser and hated me. She said I was stupid and fat."

My thoughts whirled. The Rev was supposed to be teaching us important aspects of living a well-balanced, fulfilling, and healthy life, yet here she was telling me she had been a victim her whole life. I was speechless, astounded that she had chosen to reveal such a weakness with me. Why be so candid about her private life and innermost insecurities? Her emptiness and sadness filled the space between us with heaviness. Hoping to convey my sympathy, empathy, and understanding, I reached out and touched her arm. But in truth, I didn't have a clue about how to help this poor, lost woman.

Her cigarette was still burning, and I could see the long ash was ready to drop at any moment. Neither of us said a word, but I couldn't stop staring at the glowing embers. Every day she reminded all of us that she did readings for a hundred bucks an hour and that we should all be sure to schedule a reading with her. We laughed behind her back, wondering how in the world she could think any of us would want to have a reading with her. She hadn't really given us the consistent impression that she knew what she was doing. We did know she was trying wholeheartedly to help us connect with our angels. She said she wanted to show us the magic of the dolphin spirit energies. But she also said if we didn't behave, the dolphins wouldn't come, which made us feel like small children being reprimanded for not following the rules.

But now after seeing her so vulnerable, I was a bit more curious about her readings. I wanted to make her feel better in whatever small way I could, so I asked if she had time tomorrow after lunch to do a reading with me. She explained that she would be channeling her spirit guides from centuries past. They would merge with mine and begin to set me free from whatever was holding me back in life. I nodded and then trudged with a heavy heart back to our group. This poor, pathetic woman had let her guard down and exposed her vulnerability to me. She assumed that I was the ringleader of our group. She had built a bridge between us, and I didn't want to break it. So I chose not to tell my friends what had transpired. I couldn't. It was all so empty and sad. I returned to my friends, who were still uproariously laughing together. They all gathered around to ask if everything was all right. I told them that it was indeed the Rev and that her path to her room was dark and overgrown with tree roots. It was difficult to navigate in the dark, so I helped her up. She said she was just fine, just a bruised ego for falling and screaming so loudly. I wondered how the path to the Rev's room would look and feel the next day once the sun was shining.

8

The next day as I approached the Rev's room, I was relieved and comforted to see the huge banyan tree that towered over her hut enveloping it under its strength and beauty. I felt some peace knowing she woke every morning and fell asleep each night enfolded within its branches.

I stood outside her door and waited, remembering she liked to nap (or meditate, as she called it) in the late afternoon. Besides, I didn't want her to yell at me the way she had yelled at Jeanne and Kat for singing in the showers during her nap. The stifling smell of cigarette smoke leaked from one of her windows, so I knew she was awake. I still hadn't recovered from the fact that she smoked. My mind wandered, imagining monks with long white cigarettes in their hands and smoke puffing from their mouths like chimneys. What a comical mental picture! I pondered the thought did monks smoke?!!

Her door was just a thin sheet of bamboo hanging in the doorway. As I was looking for something to knock on, her commanding voice boomed from within, causing me to jump. "Just push it aside and enter."

Somewhat hesitantly, I moved the bamboo sheet aside

and crossed the threshold into her room. She was sitting on her bed and patted the space next to her. After I sat, she poured us some tea while simultaneously squashing out her cigarette butt in a beautiful shell ashtray. Thank God she put her cigarette out before my reading began. Next she told me to lie on the bed and start doing my breathing exercises. She led me through a meditation that was more poetic than her usual circle ceremony prayers, and for a moment I wondered if she had broken some kind of barrier between us. Maybe this reading wouldn't be that bad. Feeling more accepting toward her, I let my guard down, hushed my inner critic, and forced my monkey mind to be still.

Then the reading started. She jabbered on about how in a past life I was a priestess before finally becoming a queen who ruled an entire city—the city of Atlantis! *Oh brother, here we go*, I thought. *Couldn't she be more creative than queen of Atlantis?* She told me I have a strong connection to children and animals, a great love and respect for all living things. She then changed direction and asked me to tell her the dark thoughts I had been harboring like a "heavy piece of stinkin' shit" since I was a little girl. Her harsh swearing and sudden intensity was confusing and uncomfortable. She kept telling me to expose the evil, unveil the truth, and get rid of the wickedness I carried. It was time to release and let it all go. I shook my head and mumbled as if in a catatonic state, trying to follow her lead but also hoping to direct her away from this angry garbage about pulling out my evil. "I really don't have any unhappy or bad childhood memories," I murmured.

She took a deep breath in, let it out, and rubbed the side of my arm. I took a deep breath too, trying to calm myself and rein in the giggles that wanted to burst out of me. *Shit, where is this going?* I wondered. I imagined popping straight up and shouting, "Are you kidding me? I'm paying you one hundred dollars for *this*?" Just imagining it made me want to laugh.

Suddenly and abruptly, she yelled at the top of her lungs, "Let the devil out! It is evil! It corrupts you!" Completely taken aback, I opened one eye and peeked at her bright red face, her cheeks all puffed up. *Oh my God! Please don't make me have to do CPR on this lunatic,* I thought. "Dig deeper! Deeper!" she continued, little flecks of spit flying from her purple lips. "Find this foulness that fills you! Something happened to you in your past that you haven't been able to let go of! It will eat your insides and create an unhappy future! What is it? Tell me now!"

She brought her hands together in one thunderous clap that made me jump. My heart was racing, and I went from being a bit scared to completely terrified of this crazy woman. Desperately, I began racking my brain to connect with this awful, ugly thing that was supposedly causing me so much angst and evilness. Could it be stealing clothes when Jeanne and I were fourteen? Maybe the Rev was referring to all the lies I tell myself? Was it that I'm not always truthful with myself and others? No, none of those seemed right, so I discarded them along with a few other possibilities. Ultimately, I reached the conclusion that I was healthy enough to not let past mistakes bog me down. That satisfied me, but she was relentless.

"Shout with me now, Misha!" she commanded. *"Fuck! Fuck! Fuck!"* Reluctantly, I cursed aloud with her. "Now tell me what it was that was so terrible! You need to unburden the shackles!"

Suddenly, my mind drifted back to the abortion I had when I was sixteen. I had thought I was at peace with it, but maybe I wasn't after all. I knew the Rev needed something big, so I decided to serve her this and see where it went. In an effort to escape her heated breath on my face, I moved over on the bed. When I mentioned my abortion, you would have thought she was having an orgasm from the moans and groans. She began rocking back and forth with her eyes closed, ordering me to say, "Fuck," over and over again, but I was never loud enough for her. Despite my use of other four-letter words, this word felt uncomfortable passing over my lips. I hardly ever even whispered it in my imagination. I had children, and letting a word like that slip wasn't ever called for. I was sweating. She was sweating profusely too! When her body odor started to choke me, I finally yelled out of sheer frustration "*Fuck!*" This time it was loud enough to satisfy her.

"Yes, yes, yes, *yes*!" she cried. After saying a prayer, she suddenly excused herself, leaving me there on the bed, bewildered and alone like a boat lost at sea after a storm. Was this just another absurd happening in what had become a somewhat absurd spiritual retreat? After a moment, I smelled cigarette smoke. She was outside smoking a cigarette! I'd had enough. I got up and made for the door, but as I crossed the doorway, the Rev's heavy arm came down across my chest, stopping me in my tracks. "Rather than money, can you pay me with marijuana? I know you ladies have some," she said. Lord in heaven, this was unreal.

"Fine," I said. "But I don't have a hundred dollars' worth."

"Well, whatever you can get will be fine." I left and returned with a small stash for her. Then I went to search for my friends. There was no way I could tell them about all this yet. I didn't know whether to laugh or cry.

9

The next morning we went through what we refer to as "the chain gang event." The Rev said she'd wake us before dawn. She'd blindfold us and lead us by our hands down a narrow path to the water's edge. We would arrive at sunrise to witness the dawn in all its splendor and glory, a vision like we had never witnessed before. For some reason, I believed her and actually felt my heart stir at the thought of participating in this activity.

Sure enough, the Rev showed up in our rooms at three in the morning. Even though it was pitch-black outside, blindfolds were placed over our eyes. She linked our hands together and talked to us about trusting the hands we were holding. She took the lead with a flashlight in one hand and my hand in the other. "No talking!" she told us. "Walk holding the hands in silence!"

The Rev yanked me forward, and we were off. As we stumbled along, we suffered a few stubbed toes. Torey in particular was upset because she was so short that the person in front of her was pulling her forward while the person behind her was pulling her backward.

I kept my silence, intent on following the Rev closely and not tripping. She had the only flashlight. At one point, I thought she was going to lead us all over a cliff. I stifled a laugh at the thought of such a crazy idea. Then I took a sharp breath with a slight flush of panic—anything was possible with an unstable person like the Rev.

After stumbling through the dark for what felt like miles, we finally reached our destination. At last, we could remove our blindfolds and release one another's hands. The experience of totally trusting the hands we were holding was surprisingly profound and exhilarating. Then to open our eyes and behold the sight before us was beyond words. We were at the edge of a towering cliff where hundreds of sea turtles were swimming in the ocean sprawled out beneath us. A whole community of turtles—mommies, daddies, grandparents, babies, aunts, and uncles—were feeding at this particular inlet, letting the waves leisurely jostle them around.

The moon was lost behind a thin, opalescent layer of clouds, and the glowing sunrise painted the sky in electric pinks and golds. The streams of colored light were so pronounced we could have stood in one shaft of light and claimed it as ours alone. Bursting with joy at the beauty of it all, my friends and I lined up and held out our arms under the shafts of light. I felt as if we were under a maypole with shiny, multicolor ribbons blowing in the air. It was an amazing sight to behold.

Layne used this moment to share with us what she knew about auras. She explained that when we walk into a room and then immediately feel certain energies, those feelings are created by people's auras—the energy fields that surround all living things. Auras strongly influence when we feel an immediate connection with someone or when we feel chills from someone else. Some people are born with the ability to view auras easily, while others can learn to view them over time. When we are equipped with the understanding of our own auras, we can use them to learn more about ourselves and how we relate to others. Layne moved on to discuss the meanings of different aura colors and how to strengthen and protect our auras. She closed this class with information about our chakra energy system and the fact that every person has a golden rod within them that connects and grounds them to the earth.

As Layne spoke, I thought about my daughter Bryn, who was four years old. I swear Bryn could see auras everywhere. We would be riding our horses through the forest together—she on her little white pony named Cosmos and me on Sai Moon. She would point and say things like "Oh, look at all the colors around that fern!" or "Look at that tree's lightness!" At first, I attributed this to her innocence, but as she grew older, she never lost this insight. She saw the light in everything and created the most phenomenal artwork for someone her age. She had a remarkable childhood gift, and many years later she has managed to retain it.

I was snapped back from these memories by Reverend Faith's harsh voice interrupting Layne. The Rev said that a person could sever another person's golden rod with words of hatred, bitterness, and evil. One hateful person could send another spiraling out of control, which is one reason why so many people are on antidepressants nowadays. Then she lit a cigarette! The Rev continued to stand close to Layne, who had her eyes closed and chin lifted toward the sunrise. After all we had seen and experienced, I still couldn't believe she had the audacity to light up a cigarette right now, of all moments.

"Are you in the same dream I'm in right now?" Kat asked, looking at me in disbelief.

"This isn't a dream. It's a nightmare," Torey mumbled.

"It is what it is," said Jeanne in a motherly tone.

Ziggy smiled and mumbled, "I will never forget this trip for as long as I live."

I remained silent, shocked because Reverend Faith had started waving her hand back and forth through the middle of Layne's golden rod while still holding her cigarette in her other hand. *What the heck is going on?* I thought.

Ziggy also watching the Rev's antics and said, "I feel like I'm going to throw up again."

Torey was rubbing her shoulder and complaining that it had been dislocated during our blindfolded walk when the Rev, who was still waving her hand through Layne's golden rod, hissed and said, "Shhh!"

"This is all such BS," Torey whispered under her breath.

Choosing to look away from the Rev and focus on the positive, Kat seemed mesmerized by the beauty of the sunrise. She had the majesty and grace to create her own little space of calm. When I inched closer and reached for her hand, she gave me a little wink and a warm smile. It was such a comfort to have friends on my same wavelength who processed life in a similar way as me.

Our exultation in the rising sun was again jolted by a shriek that came from the Rev. Out of the blue, she exclaimed, "Layne is now firmly grounded in the earth! Tomorrow we will swim with the dolphins! So be it … *now*!" Then she stomped her foot.

Dear God. I raised my eyebrows at Jeanne, who was pursing her lips to keep from giggling. At least we had one another to cling to amid the strangeness and confusion of this trip. Like being on a roller coaster, the ups and downs of each day had us dizzy and sometimes overwhelmed with doubt. If it weren't for our unconditional love for one another and knowing we had one another to lean on, the negatives would have overwhelmed the positives.

We walked back to our hut together, quiet and

introspective. In the back of my mind, I heard a familiar bit of cosmic wisdom. "Know thyself, and to thine own self be true." I couldn't remember who'd said that, but the words resonated with me. Then another familiar phrase came to me. "Become what you want to attract, and all things good in life will follow." When we reached the minibar in Torey and Kat's room, something inside us broke. We all fell on the beds, rolling with laughter, tears streaming down our faces.

"What the hell just happened?" I asked. Nobody had an answer. All we knew was that despite the craziness, today had been a special day because we were finally going to swim with dolphins. We couldn't wait for our next adventure.

At lunch an island celebrity came to talk to us about our upcoming swim with the dolphins. Her name was Terry, and once we met her, we concluded that she was the angel we had been searching for since we'd arrived at the retreat. Terry had the softest cadence in her speech, fluid body movements, and the spirit of a truly genuine, kindhearted woman. She was in great shape and had long blonde hair that had bleached from spending her days under the Hawaiian sun. Indeed, she was sun-kissed.

After lunch Terry brought us to Queen's Pond for Watsu, which was going to help prepare us for tomorrow's swim with the dolphins. Queen's Pond was a freshwater pond the size of a football field where an ancient Hawaiian queen supposedly came to bathe. A cliff covered in hanging orchids was behind us, and a cement wall at the other end faced the ocean and sandy beaches. Eucalyptus and giant palm trees flanked our sides, and a small tributary flowed into the pond, allowing some salt water to gently mingle with the fresh water. We felt like we were floating on the edge of the world.

When we put our fins and masks on, we could see small schools of fish, turtles, and other marine life among the mossy rocks below. We were swimming around and enjoying the natural beauty and wildlife when Terry entered the pool, ready to begin Watsu. She explained that she was a certified Watsu instructor and had spent literally hundreds of hours training in the proper therapy and instruction techniques. "For those of you who haven't experienced Watsu, it is a form of aquatic therapy," she explained. "It combines massage, muscle therapy, muscle stretching, and dance into specific movements that are usually performed in warm water by an instructor and a receiver. Today I will be the instructor and you will take turns being the receiver. You can expect me to completely support you while you float. I will cradle your body, rock you, and massage and stretch your muscles. This is primarily a relaxation exercise, but Watsu's specialized movements and stretches also offer a range of therapeutic and healing benefits. By alternating moments of stillness with rhythmical flowing movements, we can free the body in ways that are impossible on land. The warm water will relax your muscles while supporting your spine and freeing your body from its own weight. This allows your back, joints, and muscles to be easily manipulated and freed in a way unique to water therapy. By the end of this exercise, you should feel the very gentle yet deep effects of the stretching, an equally deep state of relaxation, free of all stress and tension."

Each of our sessions would last for about an hour. I volunteered to go first. Terry said I needed to trust her to move my body. After she promised not to let my nose go underwater until I was ready, she started slowly, holding me under my arms and cradling my head between her breasts. I looked dreamily up at the sky. We were surrounded by humongous trees whose branches reached over the water, casting lacey shadow patterns throughout the pond. Blue and yellow birds were flittering above, hopping from branch to branch. Cupping my chin with her hand, Terry gently submerged the back half of my head while keeping me afloat with her knees. Initially, I didn't like the feeling of water flowing into my ears, but then she reminded me to just relax, let go, and allow her to move my body. She slowly rocked me back and forth, sometimes pulling me into her arms and cradling me like a baby before softly pushing me out into the warm, soothing water. Soon I was putty in her hands. I was as relaxed as a wet noodle. Her movements replicated a dance that was so fluid and seamless that I lost all sense of time and direction. All sound was muted by the water, and I just rested within this blissful state of being.

Total trust was imperative. Terry could judge from my breathing and agility how I was doing. It was as if we came together, listening to the same music. She was the conductor, indicating with a tap of her finger when to take a deep breath and close my eyes. Then with grace and precision, she would carefully submerge me and twirl me underwater like a ballerina that was as light as a feather. My spine became like liquid motion, relaxed in a way I'd never imagined possible. The feeling was so exquisite that I wanted to stay underwater forever. As she pulled me in close, rocking me like a baby, I relaxed into the flow and allowed the movement to enfold me. I can't explain it, but tears began streaming from my eyes. It was like being back in my mother's womb in a state where time stood still. During those moments in Terry's arms, I glimpsed the true meaning of bliss. It felt like I was in my mother's womb once again. The feelings were undeniable. I had found my mom. She was talking to me. She was my angel.

In a gentle voice, Terry instructed me to slowly open my eyes. As my eyelids parted, the afternoon sunlight gleamed like a sparkling diamond. I couldn't speak. I didn't want to ever leave this space. After gently placing me on a rock, Terry swam over and took Jeanne's hands next, bringing her into the same peaceful, sacred space I was in. Jeanne relaxed immediately, allowing the tears to pour from her eyes from beginning to end. I watched, mesmerized, witnessing what I had just been feeling.

Kat and Torey recognized the space I was in and allowed me to bask in the sunshine on the rock Terry deposited me on. I drifted off to sleep and woke to find mermaid tears flowing down my cheeks. Kat took her turn after Jeanne. She looked beautiful in the dwindling afternoon sunlight, as graceful as the dragonflies flitting over the orchids and as fluid as liquid gold. The sunlight danced above, beneath, and around her beautiful, feminine form.

Ziggy's beauty was always a breathtaking sight to behold. Releasing her ponytail, she shook out her long blonde tresses and reached for Terry. She opened herself up effortlessly spreading her arms, as an eagle might, soaring and skimming through a gentle breeze.

Torey went last. She seemed a bit hesitant initially and then mumbled, "Oh, what the heck." After learning that Torey didn't like her ears getting wet because she couldn't stand the feeling of water trickling into them, Terry swam over to her backpack and pulled out a set of earplugs, which Torey placed carefully in her ears. But she didn't particularly care for the feel of the earplugs either and questioned who else had worn them before her. Terry reassured her they were brand-new. In fact, she only brought them for people like her who didn't like water in their ears. When her session started, Torey was stiffer than the rest of us had been and was having a difficult time relaxing and going with the flow. While we had allowed our bodies to become like ribbons trailing in the water, Torey's remained rigid. Terry spent a lot of time just swaying and rocking Torey back and forth as if she were in a bunting blanket until a slight but content smile finally came to her lips. Eventually, she closed her eyes.

After our amazingly relaxing Watsu experience, the other girls chose to take the main path back to the retreat while

Jeanne, Terry, and I decided to take a different trail that was lined with trees, black lava rock, and black sand back to our places. As the three of us walked, Terry stopped and reached down to pick up a quartz crystal the size of my baby finger and placed it into my palm. I stared in awe. Its beauty absolutely took my breath away. After a few more steps, Terry reached down to pick up another crystal. It was a little smaller but just as beautiful. This one she pressed into Jeanne's upturned palm and said, "How perfect for the two of you."

As the three of us embraced, I searched but couldn't find any words, just a heartfelt silence and connection with everyone and everything. I had never been afraid to venture across new horizons, and now with its abundant gifts and exquisite elements at our feet, the earth overwhelmed me. My wonder was a fragile soap bubble, and I dared not pop it.

10

Every night in the sacred rice circle, everyone diligently lit a candle for our guardian angels. Afterward, we brought them back to our rooms. We cherished these candles. Each time we lit them, we received inspiration and hope that we would find what we were looking for here after all—despite realizing this retreat wasn't exactly what we had expected.

Our obsessive care over our candles reminded me of times when my children each had to carry an egg around with them for a week as part of a school project. *Don't break it. Bring it to school every day. Make a bed for it. Bring it to the breakfast table and the dinner table.* They had to take their eggs to soccer practice and outside when they were playing. They had to keep it next to them when they were playing video games too. At first, I thought trying to teach our children the responsibility of caring for something 24-7 was crazy. A full week seemed like too much, especially since I ultimately became the eggs' mother too. I was always hovering around my kids, reminding them to take proper care of their eggs. So obviously, it was just too much for *me*. The egg didn't make it the full week with any of our children. Our daughter, the artist, painted a face on her egg and dressed it up in a cute outfit. When the boys cracked theirs in their backpacks or during games of catch in the TV room, it saddened our youngest son. The night before his egg cracked, I listened to him telling his egg a bedtime story about how it was going to grow up to be a beautiful rooster. He was so sensitive that I worried about his heart bruising over the loss of that egg. Our youngest son, Koll, has always had a joyful and tender heart and a profound sensitivity.

Similarly, we grew attached to these candles that represented our angels. As women, we nurtured and embraced the seeds we planted for our angels whenever we lit the wicks. We wanted so much for our angels to reveal themselves and guide us on our lifetime journeys.

I performed the candle ritual every day, personally believing that our angels would visit us in our dreams, where they could reach our unconscious minds more readily than our conscious minds. One night I shared an experience with the group that I believed was my first angel encounter. That experience had left me with an unshakable belief in angels—or at least in an all-encompassing, loving energy that constantly surrounded us.

It happened a few weeks after Laef, our first son, was born. I was breastfeeding, and I'd been waking at all hours of the night to feed him. Awakened one early dawn by his snuffling cry for milk, I semiconsciously pried my exhausted body from my bed to pick him up from his cradle. Zombielike, I shuffled toward his room to nurse him and change his diaper.

When I reached the door, I noticed a soft light gleaming from the crack under the door. *What the heck?* I wondered. I knew it wasn't a full moon. Yet the light danced from beneath his door like a ray of sun underwater. Opening and closing my eyes several times, I stopped and just stood staring, not believing what I was seeing. Laef's little body cradled safely in my arms, the newborn baby scent of his blankie tickling my nose, I suddenly felt very alive. My senses heightened, I breathed in his essence, still so fresh from heaven.

As I walked into Laef's room—into the land of teddy bears, giraffes, musical toys, colorful mobiles, and wooden rocking chairs—I wasn't afraid of the presence that seemed to fill the room. I sat in the wooden rocking chair, my baby suckling my breast, and then I saw the light outline of a male entity. Radiating love, his arms were opened as wide as the room, and he was as tall as the ceiling. I knew beyond all doubt that this presence was guarding and blessing our new baby's room, as well as his newborn soul. Mesmerized, I sent my unconditional love to this effervescent light. I absolutely knew this was our child's guardian angel. I could *feel* it. As his radiant love and goodness permeated the room, I promised myself I would keep this truth sacred and close to my heart always. With our other two children, I often felt this boundless love encompassing their rooms as well.

When Laef began talking, he would jabber, jabber, jabber all the time. Once I heard him say, "Okay, does that sound like a good idea for you?" When I asked him who he was talking to, he said, "Jake, of course."

"Who is Jake?" I asked.

He looked at me as if I had two heads and said, "You know! My best friend!"

"Where is he?"

"Right here in front of us," my son replied as he spread his arms wide, trying to span from one corner of the ceiling to the other. When I asked Laef to explain Jake to me, I learned that he was huge, he never got mad, he always laughed, and he was *always* there. There was my son, who was so little, and there was this giantlike, seemingly bigger than life, a constant best friend to comfort and protect him.

For some reason, Jake stopped hanging around just before

my son started kindergarten, and I felt his absence long after he was gone. Once I asked about Jake. My son just shrugged and said, "Oh, we don't talk that much anymore, but he is still here. Sometimes when I think I feel him, I wonder if he's just pretend."

It hurt me to see this loss of innocence in my son. A few days later, my sweet little boy handed his teddy bear to me after I tucked him in and kissed his precious face good night. "Here, Mom," he said. "Take Teddy. I don't really need him anymore."

My mouth flew open as a mist of tears clouded my eyes. "No, honey, but Teddy really needs *you*, so you should keep him in bed safe with you all night." Laef agreed to take Teddy back, but it pierced my heart to see him hide Teddy under his pillow instead of cuddling him up under his neck. Teddy is now safe in my hope chest with other baby treasures.

So anyway, those were my angel experiences before the retreat. When I shared this story with my friends, their responses weren't what I expected, but it didn't matter. Despite what they thought about it, they still loved me. And I still clung to what I knew in heart to be true. I knew our children had angels—*big* ones—watching over them. As do we all.

Over the years I had often replayed these angel memories, but each time the feelings and knowledge faded a little more. It had taken me months before deciding to share these events with my husband. I knew that Craig (as the analytical skeptic he was) would try to burst my fragile bubble of belief, and I feared that the feelings would simply evaporate. As a scientist, he loved to play the devil's advocate. He was very skeptical and questioned anything outside the box. I realized that over our years together, I had been quietly judgmental and maybe even disdainful of his lack of acceptance for the spiritual side of life.

I wished I could help him see how an angel's goodness beat all evil and understand how believing in positive spirits or energies could be a constant positive force in his life. I wanted to show him the world through my eyes for a change—sky, stars, sunshine, nature, snowflakes, seasons, babies, marriage, love, happiness, imagination, and beyond. From my perspective, Craig's stubbornness had kept him bound up like a slave in chains. I knew that his upbringing had made him the man he was—that his Norwegian DNA had to play some part in both his brilliance and his stubbornness. But then I wondered if maybe he loved me *because* he could see the world through my eyes but would never admit it. Maybe he needed me around to *show* him.

With that sudden realization, I saw the beautiful tapestry of our lives. My wonderful husband and I had woven it together over the years with threads of love, respect, and admiration. Sure, there were some holes here and there where we may have pushed too hard in different directions, but it was no less impressive. I thought about us resting in each other's arms under the blankets of our bed at the end of the day. There was peace. He was where I belonged forever. Until death do us part.

11

Another amazing day was about to unfold. Today we were finally going to swim with wild dolphins! I woke with such excitement I could hardly contain myself. We were going to a bay where the dolphins came to rest after feeding all night. Ready to get moving, I rounded up my friends.

When we reached the bay, we met Terry. She first taught us to enter the water in a conscious state of grace, love, or joy so as to send positive, inviting energy to the dolphins. "Center yourselves before you leave the beach," she said. "Use silence, movement, breath work, chanting, meditation, or whatever it takes for you to reach your center."

Still resonating from the kindness, light, and understanding of our Watsu sessions with Terry the evening before, we trembled with anticipation as we listened to her instructions. Before entering the water, she reminded us to respect the dolphins' space and habitat and to tune into their energy. We each teamed up with a buddy and then slowly swam out into the bay with deliberate intentions and the highest of hopes that we would have a dolphin encounter.

It was a cool day, and the bay was choppy with a somewhat

chilling breeze. The clouds crawled lazily across the overcast sky, only occasionally letting a ray of sunlight break through. As Terry guided us to deeper waters beyond the bay, I was enchanted by the wave patterns in the sand and the numerous schools of fish swimming below us.

Torey kept having equipment problems. Her face mask was leaking, and her fins were too big, even though I had put a pair of socks on her tiny feet and cinched her fins as tight as they would go. She had also started getting a blister on one heel, and it was annoying her so much that she wanted to take her fins off. Terry strongly encouraged her to push past the discomfort, saying it would go away soon, but eventually, Torey took the fin off her blistered foot and swam with only one. Then her face mask kept getting foggy, and Jeanne kept helping her spit into it, adjust it, and get her hair out of it— one thing after another. But the mask just wasn't connecting to her face enough to get the suction it needed, and she complained that it was giving her a headache. Kat was her partner, so she stayed behind with Torey while the rest of us swam farther out.

Suddenly, we heard the unmistakable sound of a whale call. Terry began treading water and waited for us to gather around her. When she told us to put our heads in the water and listen, we distinctly heard the whales singing and calling to one another. She told us to look out at the horizon. There in all its glory was a pod of four and then five and then six—more than a dozen beautiful whales leisurely swimming across the ocean's edge. What an overwhelming sight!

Once the whales disappeared beyond the waves, we forged on. As the wind picked up, hitting the tops of the cresting waves, a fine mist sprayed from the whitecaps into our faces, and then we heard it! It was the sound we had been waiting for—the playful chattering of dolphins. My heart fluttered in unison with their chitchat. Terry could tell from the sound that it wasn't a big pod—maybe ten or so. We scanned the horizon, searching for dorsal fins or some other sign of their whereabouts. Just the sound of their echolocation was extraordinary! They sounded so close, but we couldn't see them.

Then suddenly, we saw them on the surface within swimming distance. Forgetting all about our fogging masks, blisters, ill-fitting fins, and the cold, we kicked our feet as fast as we could. Terry swam steadily toward the pod with us in tow. Just the exuberance of our own pod was extraordinary. Our energies were all connected, and I kept getting waves of goose bumps. But whenever we started to get close to the dolphins, they would swim off in another direction. At one point, we couldn't hear them at all. I wondered if in our excitement our energy levels might have risen way above what a dolphin would respond to. Terry reassured us that the dolphins were still near. If we just stayed with them in our hearts and our minds, they would reappear.

Layne and Reverend Faith had stayed behind, and I could see them on the shore, shading their eyes as they watched us. I knew they could also see the dolphin pod. Once every few minutes, a few of the dolphins would flip out of the water, spinning through the air in a playful show of glee. But they seemed to be getting farther and farther away from us.

After a while, my friends grew disappointed as the sound of the dolphin's chitchat became increasingly distant, and they decided to swim back to shore and return later. But I wasn't ready to leave yet. Fortunately, Terry was my buddy, so while everyone else swam back to shore, we stayed out. I gave her a thumbs-up and a huge smile, we continued swimming toward the faint dolphin chatter we could still hear in the distance. When we finally found the dolphins again, Terry looked at me over her shoulder and put a finger to her lips, signaling for quiet. I was right beside Terry, our shoulders nearly touching when she signaled for me to stop. She pointed directly below us. As I looked down, the thumping of my heartbeat pounded in my ears and throat. There they were—three beautiful dolphins. One very large dolphin, one medium, and one tiny baby were all swimming beneath us. Terry popped her head up out of the water and indicated for me to do the same. "I've seen these dolphins before," she said with a smile. "That little guy is the baby, and there is his mother. The big one is the auntie."

She whispered for me to be still and enjoy the wonder. The dolphins were skimming over the ocean floor less than fifteen feet below us. My body felt warm all over. As the little family kept a watch on us, I made eye contact with each of them. I, of course, was mesmerized by the baby. He and I locked eyes, and the next thing I knew, he was darting up toward us! Trying to control my energy level and calm my racing heart, I took a few slow, deep breaths. Suddenly, the auntie dolphin jetted up in front of the baby and bounced her nose against his head, causing him to swim right back down to the ocean floor. It all happened so fast! This same scenario happened three more times. Terry popped her head up to tell me that the aunt was scolding the baby, who was just curious and wanted to check us out. I was witnessing an auntie educating her nephew how to interact with humans.

Once while she was blocking the baby from getting too close to us, the auntie actually brushed against my calf. It was beyond anything I had ever felt in my life. Making no waves, I lifted my head out of the water and looked at Terry, silently clapping my fingers together in excitement. What I really wanted to do was leap for joy, clap loudly, and squeal with delight. Terry reached over and grabbed my hand, pointing down as all three dolphins darted toward the surface at lightning speed. They leaped into the air, spun 180 degrees, and then slipped fluidly back into the water. Then the baby began circling under our legs and the two females came up within an arm's reach of us. Popping their heads out of the water, they clapped their fins (mimicking me) as they chattered back and forth with each other.

It was all so amazing I wanted to cry, but I knew it would mess with my face mask. So I just kept breathing it all in with awe and respect. All three of our dolphins did a few more jumps and spins, and then they just took off, disappearing beyond the waves. I looked at Terry, ripped my face mask off, and jumped into her arms, enfolding her in a wild embrace. We laughed aloud, and I yelled, "Yahoo!" From ashore we heard laughter, cheers, and clapping. Everyone had witnessed the whole thing. When we swam back onto the shore, my friends ran into the wake to greet us. Just witnessing our experience with the dolphins had filled their hearts too. They felt like they had been right out there with us.

Feeling a need to protect this special time and keep it to myself just for a bit longer, I was very introspective that afternoon and evening. I knew I'd been so blessed to have connected with the dolphin family, and I was also grateful to my dear friends for giving me the space I needed to process the whole experience. As I contemplated the feelings and emotions this amazing day had unleashed, I remembered a time when my daughter Bryn and I were riding our horses in the forest behind our house. We had heard on the news that a great white owl had been sighted near our area, which was way outside of its normal territory of Alaska and Canada. We were riding along quietly when all of a sudden, she stopped in front of me and said, "Oh, Mommy, look!" Sitting on the limb of an evergreen not even six feet from us at eye level sat the most beautiful bird I had ever seen! Brushed in beautiful shades of white, silver, and taupe, it looked like it was three feet tall. Its enormous golden eyes stared unblinkingly back at us. Frozen, neither of us said a word. This moment was sacred, and we didn't want to break it. When Bryn's pony inched forward a bit, our brief connection with the majestic owl was broken. It swooped down from its branch and flew away. As it glided through the branches of the forest trees, its wings made a *whoosh, whoosh* sound. It wasn't a loud sound, but it sent a gush of wind toward us, making our hair fly from our faces.

We all have a part to play in maintaining the delicate balance of nature and beyond. For some reason, reflecting back on these two sacred moments, one with the dolphins and the other with the owl, brought me an extreme sense of peace. These two experiences were almost as enlightening and ethereal as the births of my three children. I like to think of myself as a free spirit who attracts these magical experiences to my life. I believe in rhymes and reasons. I am determined to own my truth and share it with others.

12

I shared an internal strength with my dear friends at the retreat. We were all attempting to live in the now, and we each contributed to one another's grace. Whenever one of us fell off the ship, the others would throw out a buoy to keep her afloat—a buoy to keep her head above water whenever negative thoughts interrupted her journey toward finding her destiny. We'd all had expectations for the trip. I encouraged the girls over and over again to drop all expectations and quit imagining how the trip could have been. We needed to enjoy what we had right then and there, to align ourselves with the fullness of our own individual possibilities, and to let our expectations go. This was a huge feat for anyone to accomplish, a feat that could set a spirit free. *Let go of expectations!* That's much easier said than done. Throughout the retreat we held one another up, helping us feel safe in paradise, where the sea embraced us and lulled us to sleep under the silver light of the moon each night with its methodic rhythm. What more could we ask for?

Yet we'd each had our turn, quietly crying ourselves to sleep. I missed my husband terribly at times. One night

I tried to replicate sleeping next to him by using a pillow and a blanket. I missed the feel of his heartbeat close to mine and the comforting warmth of his body. I felt anxious whenever I thought about our three children, whom I, of course, imagined missed me terribly. I trusted that my dad, who moved in with us after my mother passed, was doing well within our household. Haunted by the memory of my late mother, I started thinking constantly about the world back at home. It seemed that whenever I was about to drown in feelings of agony and pain for the loss of my mom, an angelic entity would swoop down and fill me with bliss. I knew that the hurt of my mother's passing would be forever etched into my heart, but I had to trust that I would be okay if I let her go. She was in heaven or wherever spirit ascended to after death, and that was that.

That evening's sacred rice circle included some exercises in tantric meditation, which involved uttering tantric mantras (or sacred chants), tantric breathing, and self-reflection. The intention was to find the same clarity of mind that is invariably attained during orgasm, though tantric meditation does not involve the act of sex. It just requires a state of mind that is neither willing nor able to hold on to any thoughts at the moment of orgasm. Likewise, the objective of tantric meditation is to reach and maintain this state. Again, we were instructed not to talk for the rest of the night. As we left the rice circle, we knew something sacred had transpired that night, and we each had our own insights into a deeper part of our beings and our connection to one another. My greatest realization was profound. I knew I would never be completely alone. I had my own self, my own words and thoughts that I had complete control over. And most importantly, I knew we were all pieces of a greater whole. When I reached my bed, I fell asleep the moment my head hit my pillow.

Up before the breakfast gong the next morning, I sneaked

silently down to the kitchen to get milk for Chewy and to ask Layne if what she'd felt during our tantric meditation was as powerful as what I'd felt. She reassured me that it was truly extraordinary.

When I returned to the hut, I decided to give my dear, sweet friends the gifts my husband had made for them before we'd left for the retreat—golden dolphin charms. Craig had stayed late after work to sculpt beautiful golden dolphins with diamonds for eyes. He gave me mine on my birthday, one month before my friends and I left for Hawaii. I had never been away from our children this long, and I hadn't been away from Craig in more than a decade. I adored his gorgeous, thoughtful gift. He was blessing me on my journey of self-discovery, and I felt deeply grateful for the wonderful man I had married.

"Everyone is going to love this!" I had cried when he explained that he had a charm for each of my friends. "Thank you. Thank you so much, honey. I wish I could give all my friends a husband like you." Craig had known and loved my friends almost as long as I had. Maybe he was my angel, and he'd been right under my nose the whole time.

I'd been wearing my dolphin charm around my neck during the whole trip until Torey, who couldn't forget her experience losing her sunglasses and flip-flops, suggested I take it off and put it somewhere safe. At first, I refused, but one day after I chipped a tooth on it while flipping my hair over to blow-dry, she insisted.

It was a warm, muggy evening, and we had all decided to wear our nicer outfits to dinner—skirts and tank tops. After dinner we made the evening extra special by taking a few bottles of wine over to the stream behind our hut for an early evening drink. The waning sliver of the moon cast a soft glow over the meadow as we walked, and the soft sound of a stream trickled in the distance. Kat was leading the way when she suddenly came to an abrupt halt, squatted down over the grass, and lifted up her skirt. Torey had been following closely on her heels and didn't have enough time to stop. Tripping over Kat, she cried aloud in surprise.

I ran forward to help Torey to her feet. "Are you all right?"

Kat was peeing right there on the pathway, and I could make out her smile in the moonlight. "I just couldn't hold it in any longer."

"Aren't you wearing underpants?" Ziggy asked with a laugh.

"Hmmm," Kat said. "I guess I forgot."

I shook my head. Shaved pussy, squatting and peeing in the meadows of Hawaii under the moon's glow–how sexy our kitten was. She bounced a couple of times to "shake it off," and then she stood and said proudly, "I've taught both my daughters how to do this."

Next thing we knew, all of us were squatting and peeing. Ziggy was rather appalled at first, but eventually, even she took a firm wide stance, squatted, and let it all out. Her stream ended up being louder than the rest of ours combined.

"We have to remember this spot so we don't walk through it on our way back," Torey said as we continued toward the stream. We erupted with laughter. Torey truly was a joy to be around with her unique thoughts and her tendency to share them aloud.

When we reached the stream, we linked arms, intertwined like double-knotted pearls, and inhaled the fragrant flowers. Treading softly, we looked for the perfect spot to open the bottle of expensive wine that Torey and Kat had chosen at the liquor store. We settled upon a large rock laden with soft, velvety moss where we were afforded a perfect view of the moonlight flickering on the wet pebbles of the bank. It was another magical sight to behold—nature at its finest.

As we stained our lips from sipping the red wine, swirling its smoothness in our mouths, I realized that now was the perfect time. Reaching into the pocket of my skirt, I handed each of them a velvet drawstring pouch containing their gift from my husband. As my beloved friends—my sisters—unwrapped their golden dolphin charms with the diamond chips for eyes, all was silent except for their gasps and the beating of my heart.

I suddenly missed Craig more than ever—between my loins and deep in the pit of my stomach. As I gazed at the moon, I sent my love to him and our children, wishing with all my might I could be home with them in that moment. But he was already with us. My friends were touched. You could see the delight about their new treasures on their faces. I fell for my husband all over again, loving him with my whole being and soul.

Jeanne began to weep softly. She and I had been through lifetimes together, and she had just left a relationship that turned out to be a nightmare, filled with the type of drama often found in movies. Ziggy had just gone through her second devastating divorce. Independent Kat trusted that her man was out there but just hadn't come yet. Sweet Torey had been desperately joining matchmaking sites and dating for years, looking for that perfect man to fill the void in her heart. More than anyone else, she wanted children. She was convinced that a husband would make her life whole. These precious, delicate dolphins that Craig had made touched each of their hearts more profoundly than words could say. They symbolized the strength we needed to move forward, to reach the pot of gold at the end of the rainbow.

MICHELE ETHIER

13

The day after our dolphin experience, we went back to the beach and immediately saw hundreds of dolphins jumping into the air. As we watched them from the shore in awe, a horrified expression suddenly came across the Rev's face. "They are here again!" she cried, dramatically backing away from the shore. "They are coming to harm me!"

Jeanne looked at us. "That's it," she said. "This woman is insane. I can't handle this anymore."

Somehow, I knew the time had come for me to finally tell my friends about the night the Rev had told me about her difficult childhood, her jealousy of our group's friendship, and the reading that followed. "Okay," I began. "I hate to be the one to crack open your senses, but I had a reading with the Rev a few days ago." I wanted all of them to feel some compassion and empathy for this wounded and lost soul. I didn't want them to judge me for not mentioning this to them earlier. I don't know if I was protecting myself or them from seeing how nuts she really was. Maybe I was still holding out for some *hope* that this retreat would make a turn for the best. I also wanted them to completely understand the extent of her *craziness*. I didn't want us to judge her too harshly. But I also wanted all of us to come together in an understanding that regardless of the *craziness* at times, we all had learned from some deep and powerful experiences and that we could see the bright side of life now. Sure, we all relied on one another for some answers, but mostly, we learned more about ourselves through the reflections of one another within ourselves.

"You *what*?" Jeanne blurted out.

The others looked just as astounded. I had also been astounded when I was duped by the Rev. I should have known better at the time. My news may have been the straw that broke the camel's back because all anyone could do was stare, mouths agape. I shook my head, feeling like I was reliving the crazy experience all over again.

Torey put her arm around my shoulders. "Let's get out of this place," she said gently.

But after a moment we all agreed. It was time to move on. Kat volunteered to notify Layne and the Rev that we were packing up and leaving a few days early. I felt obligated to tell them too, but I was scared to face the Rev alone, so I just went to Layne. Tenderly folding me in her arms, she said she completely understood our need to leave and gave us her blessing.

We couldn't pack fast enough! A few of us decided to take one last outside shower while singing our lungs out. Respect was out the window at this point. Torey and Jeanne were singing so loudly it scared the birds from the trees. When our laughter got the roosters crowing, we laughed even harder.

It just so happened that my dear friend Ginger and her husband lived on another part of the island. I called to see if she could recommend a good hotel for us to check into for a few nights as our flight home was still four days away. Ginger promised she would get us into a great place. Her husband was a rancher, and his family owned properties all over the Islands.

"I've got connections," Ginger said, and though I couldn't see her face, I imagined her winking at me. Less than an hour later, she called back to tell us to meet her at the Orchid Resort. As soon as she gave Jeanne the directions, we were running off, not looking back. Fifteen minutes after making our getaway, Jeanne pulled over at a McDonald's. I couldn't fathom fast food. I knew it would just make me sick. But Ziggy and Jeanne were literally drooling as we pulled up to the drive-through window. I had to admit that their burgers and fries smelled really good. I caved and ordered a milkshake.

Our energy was renewed. It felt like the first day we'd set off on our adventure before reaching the retreat. We had faced many challenges during our time there, overcome many personal hurdles, and experienced powerful breakthroughs, and overall, we succeeded. We agreed that if all of us hadn't been there together, supporting one another as a team, none of us would have made the personal progress that we did. True, we had faced a lot of craziness, but on some level we knew we were building character.

The rooms at the hotel cost $500 per night, so we decided to squeeze all five of us into one room. We had two queen-size beds and one bathroom. To avoid the scene of five women carrying twenty purses, several suitcases, and my red Styrofoam floaty horse noodles up to the room, Kat and I went alone to check in while the others went to check out the pool.

After giving our bags to the bellhop and checking in, Kat and I went up to our room. It was spectacular! There was marble everywhere, a cozy couch, a big screen TV, glass tables, a beautiful Hawaiian flower arrangement, and a fruit basket with a card from Ginger. The card said to meet her at the pool around noon. We opened the doors to the balcony to find a glorious view of the outdoor pool and the glistening ocean beyond.

Suddenly, we heard a knock on the door. We opened it to find a sweaty, red-faced kid with two carts full of our luggage. "Jeez, ladies, are you staying for the whole year?" he asked with a laugh as he struggled to catch his breath.

"We're not sure yet," I replied, handing him a generous tip. "Thank you. Hey, by the way, do you know where we could find a joint around here?"

"I'll see what I can do," he said with a smile.

After he left, the other ladies joined us, and we turned on the stereo to let the music take us away while we went into overdrive showering, changing, and applying makeup. We were dedicating this day to sipping tropical drinks with fancy little umbrellas as a celebration of our freedom.

"Look what I brought, guys." I pulled a sheet of stick-on tattoos from my cosmetic bag. We'd never had a chance to put them on at the retreat. So we chose flowers, bumblebees, four-leaf clovers, and juicy red kisses, and we put them on with the use of the hair dryer. Feeling sassy, we hid a few on our asses. Ziggy had a sweet little orange-and-yellow butterfly peeking out from the bottom of her swimsuit. It was really sexy, but she said she didn't want anyone to see it. Torey had a red rose near her groin area, and she quickly checked to make sure it wasn't peeking out like Ziggy's.

I looked over and saw Ziggy trying feverishly to scrub her butterfly off. No soap, washcloth, or hairspray was going to remove that tattoo. "Oh, fuck it!" she finally said, dropping the washcloth. "Nobody knows me here. I don't care. I'm gonna flaunt it and act like a little slut for the day."

Jeanne opened a can of kitten food for Chewy and put together a litter box. Then we were ready to go. We were all still enchanted when we arrived at the swanky pool, which featured dolphin and swan fountains and a koi pond.

We spontaneously moaned in ecstasy when we found some lounge chairs our butts wouldn't fall through. These had actual cushions! And we also had luxurious, fluffy beach towels!

"This is what I'm talking about!" I cried.

"Yeah, we are living the life now," Torey agreed.

"Making beautiful dreams together," Kat added.

When Jeanne slipped out, I wondered where she was going until she returned with a heaping ice bucket and called, "Who wants mai tais?"

The laughter that followed was so rich and pure and wonderful for our hearts and our health.

Ginger finally arrived, wearing sheer harem pants, a pair of large Jackie O sunglasses, and a huge—I mean *huge*—sun hat that she had bought for the Kentucky derby. She was one of the most beautiful women I had ever known—inside and out. Her eyes were a beautiful turquoise, but they were not her only stunning attribute by any means. Her enthusiasm was contagious, making it impossible for each of my friends to feel anything but absolute adoration for her. Her personality was so unique, pure, and genuine. She had a tinkling laugh like that of a little girl.

When Ginger sat down with us, we couldn't help laughing as we told her about our outrageous retreat. Not as perturbed anymore, Torey joined enthusiastically in the telling of our tale. Jeanne became kind of introspective and went to sit by herself in the shade of a palm tree. She'd had a persistent cough during the course of our trip, and it seemed to be growing worse. She was aware that it was becoming annoying to Ziggy and me since we'd been sharing the same room. She really couldn't help it, and I felt so bad for her. One night Ziggy sat up straight in bed, threw her pillow across the room, and yelled, "*Stop* coughing!" Poor Jeanne. She'd even been trying to mask the sound by coughing into her pillow.

She had been trying to conquer her cough on our whole vacation.

As we carried on about our prematurely ended retreat, we didn't even notice that a group of young men in their late twenties had pulled up their chairs right next to us. Ziggy whispered not to make eye contact. We didn't want to start the strutting peacock male-female dance quite yet. We needed more peace, tranquility, and rum. But Kat could never be rude to anyone, so she greeted our new friends and asked where they were from. Soon we were altogether with them, and wow, they turned out to be the nicest, coolest, sexiest group of men!

They owned a limo service headquartered in Hollywood. Two were brothers, and the other two were their cousins. The brothers' father was a well-known Hollywood director who had bought the limo business for them, giving them some star clients, and the rest was history.

Kat and I excused ourselves to use the restroom, and of course, we immediately started asking one another if these guys were for real. In the end, we agreed they definitely seemed to be the real McCoy. When we returned, the cousin in charge of the business started showing us pictures on his phone of the guys opening limo doors for dozens of movie stars.

Poor guys, they should have shut up and stayed incognito because after three or four drinks, we were all over them like white on rice. Kat seemed to be getting along really well with the tallest brother. He had the warmest smile and the happiest eyes. His younger brother was really sweet too, and he had piercing, pale blue eyes. When he smiled, it looked like his mouth was enclosed in parentheses with an exclamation point at the end, created by a very pronounced dimple. The two cousins had longish blond hair, and the youngest one wore his in a ponytail. They were sporting Armani and Hermes sunglasses, and one was wearing a Rolex. Ha! We were in paradise with men who knew rock stars! The drinks kept coming, and we kept slurping away.

The afternoon sun began slanting through the fronds of nearby palms as we engaged in easygoing conversation. I noticed that the two brothers weren't drinking. Curious, I asked them why. They laughed. "We're on vacation!" the younger brother replied. "We have enough drugs, alcohol, and rock and roll every day in LA, so we like to take a break and relax when we come here. It's only for a few days. Life in LA is so crazy. We just need to get away once in a while. We're also on the clock. We're contracted for a prince who comes here on his yacht a few times a year. He flies us out here once in a while and either rents or buys a limo for us to drive him, his fiancé, and their friends around. They like to go to clubs and visit celebrity friends of theirs who have mansions here. Sometimes they just party on their yacht, but we have to be at their beck and call."

They left us a short while later to take the prince's fiancé and her friends shopping, but they promised to see us later. After they left, we laughed and felt so full of ourselves that we were pathetic. Torey was humiliated because she didn't get a chance to shave her legs and the polish on one of her toes was chipped.

We were taking a small snooze in the sun when the cocktail waitress came over with two buckets of Dom Pérignon champagne. "No, no, no, that's not ours," Kat protested. "We were actually just leaving. Could we please have our bill?"

"Oh, your drinks have been paid for," our server said. We'd each had at least four drinks, all of which were doubles, along with lunch.

"What? Who would pay for all our drinks?" I wondered aloud.

"The gentleman up there paid for everything," our waitress said, pointing to the penthouse suites on the top floor. "He also asked to have these bottles of Dom Pérignon sent to you."

My friends and I looked up to find a man in a white turban standing on the balcony of the largest penthouse suite. He was looking down at us with a pair of binoculars. Even though he was pretty far away, I discerned a slight smile on his face. Wow, that was creepy. He was just standing there with his binoculars, his white garment billowing around him in the breeze like he was the overlord or something.

"Who the hell is that?" Jeanne asked.

Our waitress said he was a prince from Dubai. "If you look way out in the bay behind me—I don't want to point because we're supposed to be discreet about anything concerning him—that's his yacht out there, the one with the helicopter on top."

Holy guacamole, I thought. *Are you kidding me?* It was the limo guys' prince! And he bought *us* champagne!

"Well, we can't accept this," Kat said. "Tell him thank you anyway."

"Are you kidding?" Torey cried. "How do you put a cork back into a bottle of champagne? We should drink it!" She smiled big and waved to say thank you.

"Fine, but ignore him now, you guys," Kat said, always wise. "He might expect something from us if we accept the champagne."

"Well, I hope so!" Jeanne replied playfully, picking up the bottle.

"Absolutely," Torey agreed. "He could put me into retirement."

Once our bottles were empty, we finally returned our towels to the cabana. Passing the ocean, we decided to walk along the beach. The cresting waves reflected the bright sunshine, putting soft, slightly drunken smiles on our faces. I reached out to hold Jeanne's hand, and Kat skipped up to grab my other hand. Behind us, I overheard Ziggy retelling the story of Torey's first encounter with the ocean. Torey mumbled something about how she was finally beginning to forget about the loss of her designer sandals and sunglasses. Jeanne, Kat, and I squeezed one another's hands and rolled our eyes as we giggled under our breath.

We hugged Ginger goodbye, and she promised to return the next day for more fun, frivolities, and mai tais. "Let's plan on a fancy dinner tomorrow night too," she said excitedly. "They have a couple of fabulous restaurants here at the hotel."

"Sounds like a perfect plan," Jeanne agreed.

As we drunkenly wove our way back to our room, we got lost, laughed, bumped into one another, and realized that our drinks around the pool had left us more than a little tipsy. But we finally arrived back at our room, where I immediately went to check on Chewy.

We had all fallen in love with our little rescue kitten.

She was so adorable. We could laugh and watch her antics for hours. My hands were covered with her baby scratches. Torey worried that they looked red and would grow infected, but I reassured her that my hands were used to baby kitten scratches. It just went with the territory of owning kittens.

"Maybe you should wear gloves when you play with her," Torey suggested.

"Torey, she's not a falcon with giant talons. She's an eight-week-old kitten. These scratches are superficial, and I keep them clean. *Look*," I said, pointing to a few almost healed scratches. "These ones are almost gone, and these others will disappear in a few days." We both scrutinized my hands, each of us coming to the same conclusion. They did indeed look like I'd been in a fight with a blackberry bush. With eyes wide open, we began to laugh at the same time. "Holy shit, my hands look *awful*!"

She nodded smugly. "See, I told you! They look bad."

"Hey, really, I'm not worried," I replied. "I've been here before, and these little kitten scratches will fade and be gone in no time." I reminded Torey that I had been through at least a dozen cats in my life with more than a few litters of kittens. Eventually, I convinced her that I would be fine. Synchronization with close friends was such a wonderful thing. It was comfortable. It was real.

We decided to stay in for the rest of the night, order room service, and relax. Kat and Torrey still had some wine left over, so we popped the corks. But before we could pour, Torey decided we couldn't drink wine out of the cheap bathroom glasses. She said we needed to ask room service to bring us red wine glasses because this was an expensive wine and the taste had to be savored properly. Jeanne reached for a bottle, put it to her lips, and took a swig before passing it to me "Tastes just fine to me," she said after swallowing. Then we took turns sipping from the bottle while we waited for room service.

In no time, we heard a knock on our door. But I shot Jeanne a quizzical look, thinking there was no way it was room service already. Torey had just called in the order a few minutes ago.

"None of you gave those guys our room number, did you?" Kat asked in a fierce whisper. We shook our heads as Ziggy opened the door to find our luggage boy standing with a smile on his face, holding out four joints for us. "Here," he said. "It's on the house. Maui Wowie. Enjoy."

"Looks like the tides are finally turning," Torey exclaimed after we had thanked him. A little while later, room service arrived, and we gathered together for a delicious meal with chocolate cake for dessert.

Following our meal, Jeanne suggested that we light our angel candles and have our own sacred circle where we could reminisce and share some peaceful time together. That lasted for only a few minutes before it was overtaken by hours of cake, wine, and laughter. After a while, I collapsed onto one of the beds, exhausted. Chewy began trying to climb up the side of the bedspread; however, midway up, her little claws got stuck in the fabric, and she didn't know how to free them. I chuckled a little as she tried to figure out how to climb for the first time. Reaching down, I gently lifted her up to release her claws, and then I kissed the top of her head. As Chewy immediately began purring, Torey lay down next to me. From the bathroom we heard Kat and Ziggy deciding who was going to take the first bubble bath with the hotel's relaxing lavender bath salts. I fell asleep with a purring Chewy draped around my neck.

I awoke just in time to catch a glorious sunrise. The sun was a golden globe rising beyond the horizon. I found Jeanne smoking outside on the balcony. Glancing around, I noticed everyone else was asleep in the hotel beds except for Kat, who had passed out in a velvet lounge chair. I took a seat next to Jeanne, and we quietly watched the sun climb slowly above the turquoise ocean. I took a deep breath and sighed. What a beautiful, sun-filled day yesterday was, and what a fun night it had been. I couldn't wait to do it all again.

15

Later that day an engraved invitation from his royal highness arrived at our hotel room, requesting the honor of our beauty aboard his yacht for dinner and dancing. We felt like we were in a fairy tale. "Oh, my heart be still," I exclaimed dramatically, placing my hand over my chest. Ziggy pretended to swoon, while Kat high-fived all of us! This was too much!

Our young friends were waiting by the pool when we arrived. We excitedly told them about our royal dinner invitation and spent the rest of the day in anticipation. But as evening approached, although dinner and dancing with the prince's entourage sounded fantastic, I wasn't in the right mood for some reason. Hanging out with those young LA guys all afternoon made me miss my husband more than ever. I kept dwelling on the way his touch always made me feel. I just couldn't share in the sexual tension my friends felt while flirting with our new friends. But being around the dance of female and male energies was intoxicating. They couldn't push against their natural instincts any more than they could fight the tide. It would have been like trying to stop fireworks after the spark had already been ignited. Still though, being surrounded by sexual tension all afternoon had left me craving some intimacy of my own.

In the frenzy of makeup, hair-curling, perfume, and showers, everyone seemed to be in harmony with mutual feelings of happiness and sisterhood. But while they were strutting their beauty like peacocks, I felt lost. I inhaled and smiled and then told them, "I'm not going with you tonight."

"What the hell!"

"Huh?"

"Come on! Are you crazy? We can't go without you!"

"No, you just go," I said, determined to stay firm despite my friends' pleas.

"Are you okay?" Jeanne asked with concern.

"No, not really," I admitted. "Craig and I have never been apart this long in all our marriage, and I miss him tons. I also miss Laef, Koll, and Bryn. It's like I'm missing one of my major organs or a limb. I just want to stay here tonight in this beautiful room and read my book. I brought four, and I haven't even opened a page yet. Maybe I'll order room service and have phone sex with my husband. I love all of you. You know that. I know in my heart of hearts that you love me too. So you go without me. Please. Just get outta here. Leave me alone. Have fun. Be safe. And if tonight turns out to be the best and most outrageous night of your entire lives, don't tell me … or just shoot me!"

Soon, a young boy who was part of the yacht staff knocked on our hotel room door, ready to pick the girls up. He instructed them to bring their passports.

"Huh? Why?" Torey and Kat asked simultaneously.

"Well, you never know if the captain might want to pull anchor and take you on a dream trip!"

Torey closed the door in the kid's face and said, "Just a moment please!" She pressed her back against the door and spread her arms, effectively barring anyone from entering or leaving. Staring at one another, the girls questioned this strange request. *Um, gazillionaire's yacht! Hello!* After a few moments, they all laughed, assuring one another that it would be safe. They weren't going to be sold into sex slavery or something. This prince probably just enjoyed older American women. Kat struck a compromise. They would leave their passports with the concierge and take copies with them onto the yacht. It seemed so blatantly risky, crazy, and fun. I told them that if they weren't home by one o'clock, I would send out the sheriff or something. I hugged and kissed each of them goodbye and told them to have a great time. They each reiterated their sadness that I was being so adamant about staying behind. But again, I told them I needed to talk with my husband.

Laughing, I pushed them out the door, and then my angels were off in a flutter of beauty and perfume. Finally alone, I picked up the room service menu, ordered a lobster salad, drank some wine, and drew a bubble bath while lighting my angel candle. Then I watched the clock, waiting for the kids to get into bed before calling my home sweet home. But there was no answer. I pulled out my book, a riveting novel by Barbara Kingsolver, to escape to the land of words for a little while. By the time I reached the second chapter, I dialed the numbers connected to my heartstrings again. When Craig answered, my heart skipped a beat. "Are all the kids asleep?" I asked.

"Not all," he replied. "Your daughter still thinks she needs another glass of water or a dose of me lying next to her in bed."

My intense love for both of them was reflected in my answer. "I'm sure you both need each other as much as I need you. I miss you so much, honey. I miss your smell. I miss your neck. I miss the feel of your lips on my collarbone. I miss the sound of your breathing when you roam my body with your senses. Go put Bryn to bed, and I'll call you back in about fifteen minutes."

"She misses you, honey. Talk to her." Craig handed the phone to our daughter.

"Mommy?" her little, desperate voice tore me open, and I lost all my lust from a moment ago. "I miss you. When are you coming home?"

I said I missed her too, and I asked about her kitten and our dog. How was her pony? Did she go riding with her aunt in the forest the other day as they'd planned? I told her I'd be home the next night for dinner, and that seemed to make her happy. "I love you, baby doll. Sleep tight. Don't let the bedbugs bite."

My sweet husband took the phone back and said, "I love you, honey. We all miss you. I think talking to you did the trick. She's going to bed now, so call me back."

"Okay, but don't fall asleep in bed with her," I said, regaining some of my lust. "I want to spend some time on the phone … with just you."

"Don't worry. I won't. I want to make love to you over the phone."

That was exactly what I had in mind too. I considered digging through Torey's bags to find that black vibrator. If I washed it really well, I'd be good to go. On our flight home, before letting them tell me about their extravagant evening on the prince's mega yacht, I'd tell everyone what I did. It could be one of the best and final laughs of our trip.

After Craig and I had our alone time, we said good night. As one o'clock rolled around, I realized I hadn't heard from any of my friends. I decided to go down to the bar to wait for them, and lo and behold, I found one of our limo brothers! He was sitting at the bar in white cotton pants, tan sandals, and a gorgeous blue silk shirt that was unbuttoned just enough to show a trace of his golden chest hair. "Hey!" I said. I took a seat next to him and told him about my friends partying on the mega yacht.

"Oh, don't I know it!" he said. "I was just there. They're all partying like rock stars and having the best time. They're hysterical. We've been totally entertained by all of them. Believe me, it's refreshing to see women who are so comfortable with themselves and have no inhibitions. You guys don't have to put on airs because you're all so naturally beautiful. The prince is enthralled with the bunch of you. You were missed by the way. And once we knew why you stayed behind, it just made you all the more alluring. A woman who would pass up the chance to be on a prince's yacht in favor of talking to her husband? He's a very lucky man."

"No," I corrected. "I'm a very lucky woman."

He asked me if I wanted to go out to the yacht to collect my group of Cinderellas. He had one of the prince's smaller boats, and we could go together. I didn't have on any makeup, but I had tan, sexy legs that I had just shaved smooth in preparation for tomorrow's reunion with Craig. So we hopped onto his boat and zoomed across the bay to board the three-deck water palace.

I had no idea how big the yacht really was until I was in its shadow. As we drew near, my ears picked up the sounds of familiar laughter, and my heart danced with joy. Oh, my friends were quite an attraction at the party, and I was so proud of each and every one of them. They could hold court with royalty.

My jaw dropped when my limo brother, whose name was Troy, helped me board the deck. It was too opulent—it really was—but to experience it just once in a lifetime was amazing. Though I strive for simplicity in my life, it was still fun to gaze at the ostentatious details—white leather *everywhere*, teak *everywhere*, crystal chandeliers *everywhere*. There was a gym, a sauna, several hot tubs, and a library with floor to ceiling hardbacks arranged by color. It even had one of those sliding ladders to reach the top shelves. I swooned. I could have been content to stay amid the books in the library. The smell of the books was intoxicating to me. Whenever I read, I always fanned the aroma of the pages, inhaling deeply,

Troy was giving me the tour. At one point he asked, "Elevator or steps?"

I said, "Steps, of course."

He laughed, saying that most women would have chosen the elevator. We came to the top deck where a rotating disco ball dangled over a dance floor. Sweet jazz filled the air from six enormous speakers and permeated the atmosphere. I felt extremely underdressed in my silk Hawaiian-print dress with the spaghetti straps and shark's-tooth hem. I wasn't wearing underpants though, which at least made me feel somewhat sensuous. When I left in search of the girls, I didn't think I would need them. Actually, I felt kind of sexy and adventurous without them. But when Troy gently placed his hand on my lower back, gently guiding me along, he slipped his hand down a little lower, and I was sure he noticed my lack of undergarments—or so I imagined. Maybe even he kind of wished I wasn't wearing underwear.

I looked around and spotted my friends relaxing in a nearby hot tub, all of them naked. Initially, I assumed the hot tub had red-colored lights, but then I realized they were relaxing in red wine—expensive red wine at that. In fact, it was more than $10,000 worth. They were surrounded by a remarkable assembly that included our host, the prince, our friends the limo drivers, the handsome Grecian captain of the prince's yacht, a French sommelier from Paris, a few other young men from the yacht crew, and the prince's betrothed!

She wasn't as young as one would have expected, but she wasn't old either. *Late twenties*, I mused. She was a natural lady-in-waiting, completely in her element here. She was the only person wearing a swimsuit—if what she was wearing could be considered a swimsuit. When my friends saw me, they jumped out of the tub, arms raised high, screaming in excitement. "We knew you would come!" Five beautiful pairs of breasts pointed at me. It was a man's dream, and it was all for me. What a vision! It's a vision I will hold in my heart until my dying days.

Suddenly feeling the urge to take charge, I cocked my head at them. "Okay, girls, the pumpkin is waiting. Time to leave the palace. Whose foot fit in the glass slipper by the way?" They all looked at the princess-to-be as she locked her arms around her prince's neck. The owner of the limo service said, "I've got the slipper to fit Kat's elegant foot." Ziggy had one of the cute, young deckhands fawning over her, even though he didn't speak any English. Jeanne had paired up with the yacht captain, while Torey was holding a bottle of extremely expensive wine in each hand from her place on the sommelier's naked lap. Her perfect breasts pointing at the stars overhead, Ginger stood up and proclaimed, "I have the Milky Way tonight!"

They were all obviously drunk, happy, and having the time of their lives. Crossing my arms over my breasts, I lifted my dress over my head and slipped into the floral-scented hot tub. It was almost as big as our pool at home. I wasn't as gone as the rest of my friends, so Torey said, "Come on! Catch up! Taste this wine. You won't believe it." She then playfully poured a whole bottle across my breasts. Monsieur Sommelier grabbed the other bottle and did the same, saying, "Here, a matched set." The prince threw his head back and guffawed.

So this was how the rich and famous lived. So much excess. So much waste. In a way, it seemed sad. Since I was more into giving back than indulging in extravagance,

I defined my social morals that evening. Yes, I loved the luxuriousness because it was over-the-top mind-boggling, but imagining my wonderful husband, children, and animals back home seemed sweeter than the Rothschild's wine being poured upon my breasts.

We entertained, we laughed, and we solved the world's problems. Listening to our Greek captain, our French sommelier, and our Dubaian prince was intoxicating with their lyrical ways of speaking. They asked us about sports, politics, spirituality, and our seemingly simple lives at home. They really enjoyed us. Of that I was sure. The prince thought Ginger was like a breath of fresh air. He told her that she reminded him of feelings he had had as a teenager. His betrothed was reserved, poised, very smart, extremely beautiful, and tolerant. She catered to his every need. It kind of made us want to gag, but we accepted it as a cultural difference. The prince took an interest in my unadulterated marriage and love for my husband, really wanting to know what it meant. After a few lines of cocaine, which was everywhere on the ship in crystal bowls, I did my best to explain the love my husband and I shared. It was something I hadn't put into words before, and I struggled to articulate the feelings of wholeness we gave one another and how it made us complete. I realized that we didn't have to really work at maintaining a connection. It had just happened that way. I wished I could have been more poetic and eloquent in my explanation. I truly wished everyone in the world, especially my friends, could find what Craig and I had found. The world would be such a happier place. Trying not to sound mundane, I stated with great conviction, "The bottom line is that all you need is love."

With that, we spontaneously launched into the Beatles song and sang, "All you need is love. Love. Love is all you need." Our limo boys found a harmonica and some guitars and joined in the song. As they continued to serenade us beneath the stars, I let go of all my worries, including needing to wake up and catch our flight home in the morning. Choosing to leave this fairy tale was one of the most difficult decisions of our lives. His highness implored us to stay. He planned to sail around the islands and then take his private jet to Greece. We were all more than welcome to stay for the month, he said. After all, the boat had twenty-six staterooms, cabin boys, two chefs, and Jet Skis galore. Jeanne said, "No way. I'll lose my job." Ziggy agreed. Kat hesitated, but ultimately, she realized she had houses to sell. Torey had a whole staff waiting for her iron fist to return. I had my sexy husband, my children, and my animals. It was time for us to return to reality.

We did switch to a later flight, compliments of the prince. With big hugs felt from deep within, we said our goodbyes. The wonder of our time aboard the yacht would never be replicated, but we all strive to preserve the memories in our hearts. We know we were also leaving positive impressions on the hearts of several sweet young limo service businessmen, a yacht captain from Greece, a French sommelier, a fun-loving prince, and his stunning princess.

Before we left, the prince's betrothed gave each of us an exquisite silk scarf as a gift. She wrapped the intricately woven scarves around each of our necks with kisses and tears. She was amazing. "Hey, you are going to be just fine," I told her. This was going to be her second arranged marriage. She had learned much from the first, and her prince seemed to be madly in love with her. She replied, "One can only pray and hope. I have been completely isolated from my sisters and mother back home. I envy you and your friends."

Back at our hotel room, we started packing our things into our suitcases quickly … and quietly in reverence to what we had just experienced. We reflected upon the roller coaster of emotions our trip had generated—ups, downs, anger, frustration, hurt, pain, happiness, and most of all, love. Last night was like a hazy dream, and we didn't feel the need to talk much. Maybe we all needed a nap or a Bloody Mary or, as Kat suggested, more of that amazing champagne. When we called the bell captain to come pick up our twenty-two bags (plus an extra that Ziggy had filled with wine from our French sommelier), one of the prince's crew members knocked on our door. We hadn't met him before, but of course, we recognized his uniform, which sported the prince's emblem. He was all serious as he said, "His royal highness would like to extend his services in transporting the ladies back to the mainland." We looked at one another, shook our heads, and figured we wouldn't fight the tides. So I placed Chewy safely into my pocket before we followed the prince's clerk to the limo that was waiting to take us (we assumed) to the airport. There they were beside the limo, our gorgeous limo boys dressed in black and white linen suits, ready to escort us. *Oh my God, will this never end?* I wondered. I hoped not. Jumping into the limo, we laughed and began popping bottles of Dom as they drove us to the airport.

Well, we had another surprise in store. We weren't going to the regular airport as we had expected. When we pulled up to a tarmac where a private Learjet was warming up its engines, we were told that this was our carriage waiting us to take us home to Seattle! By this time, we knew not to fight the tides. We'd learned to go with the flow, enjoy the ride, and thank our lucky stars. As we watched our bags being put under the belly of the jet, we high-fived, barely believing our good fortune. After we gave each of the boys a warm and heartfelt embrace, we climbed aboard. Troy patted my ass as I passed and said, "Got your panties on today, I see."

With a slight smile, I winked and said, "Oh, and here I thought you hadn't noticed."

"You have our biz cards. Call us if you ever come to LA," he said, returning my wink. "Your rides will be compliments of the house, of course. Ask for us to drive you personally. It will be our pleasure."

"Ours too," I replied.

The inside of the jet was really too good to be true. I kept pinching myself. The interior was made of leather and real gold! A kind, young hostess greeted us and offered us plates of cheese and crackers, salads, and fruits. She also offered us wine and champagne, but most of us declined, deciding it was time to drink water and take a nap, which was a struggle because the flight was a bit bumpy. The pilot was darling though. He talked to us throughout the flight in a soothing, confident voice full of humor. Kat, our gorgeous, poised, sexy kitten, went up to the cockpit to talk to him and the copilot. They even let her hold the wheel! At this point, I had seen it all—leave it to her to sweet-talk her way into their confidences.

As our flight continued, my friends relayed the events of the extravagant dinner they'd had with the prince and his betrothed before my arrival the evening before. The elaborate crystal-laden dinner table with its matching crystal candelabras and chandeliers was beyond anything they had ever seen, even in the finest of restaurants. Dressed in white linens and silks, the prince had welcomed everyone, making sure to introduce Carmen. His darling bride-to-be had been demure, reserved, and quiet yet approachable. Her demeanor suggested a genuine fondness for my brash American girlfriends, and it was obvious she adored her fiancée.

The introductions were followed by a whirlwind of caviar, salads, fruit platters, cheeses, soups, fresh lobster flown in from Maine, drawn butter, an asparagus and mushroom soufflé, and a unique veal dish with a mysterious sauce they couldn't identify. An ice sculpture made to look like a gigantic wave surrounded by a pool of ice water was the table centerpiece. A block of ice carrying oysters in the half shells lazily drifted around the sculpture. Dessert was a flaming cherries jubilee over a chocolate cake with homemade vanilla and cognac ice cream.

They were introduced to the master chef from Greece and the French sommelier. The sommelier was a big flirt who turned his ability to speak numerous languages into a game where everyone was supposed to take turns guessing what tongue he was speaking in. Our limo men were also interspersed among the prince's other dinner guests. They were beguiling everyone with stories of actors and actresses that had everyone laughing and trying to guess which celebrities they were talking about. Jeanne said they gave such vivid descriptions that it was obvious who they were referring to. Trying to guess the celebrities became a game they played at the table between courses. If someone guessed the celebrity's initials correctly, then that person was the winner and had to take a shot.

The whole party was absolutely stunning, and the girls wished they had dressed more appropriately. The prince's fiancé could speak fluently with the sommelier in every language he used. Dangling from her delicate neck was a gorgeous golden necklace featuring a rainbow set against a glowing topaz sun. The ornament was too breathtaking to be considered gaudy or fake, and Torey, who was sitting next to her, couldn't help asking about it. The prince's fiancé usually talked in a subdued voice, but even under her calm tone, it was obvious she was very happy Torey had noticed it. She humbly explained that making jewelry was a hobby of hers. She actually had a jeweler on board the yacht who helped her with her creations, which she made from jewels she'd collected from around the world. Leaning in close to Torey, she mentioned she had acquired quite the collection of rare pearls earlier that day and would love to share her treasures with Torey and "the other lady American guests."

Ziggy, Torey, Kat, and Jeanne were wearing their golden dolphin charms Craig had created. When they explained the meaning behind the gifts, the prince was transfixed, "What a genuinely thoughtful thing for a husband to do for his wife's dearest friends." He winked at Carmen. "Maybe we should do something like that for your sisters." It was an inside joke. Apparently, after announcing their engagement, they had offered numerous gifts to her mother and sisters only to have all of them returned with fervent claims that they couldn't be bought and that it was insulting to receive such gifts.

The girls were given a tour of the ship after dinner. In one of the many rooms, they found gorgeous purple leather chairs and live orchids growing from the walls with misters that went off every few minutes. After smoking from two strikingly beautiful glass Tiffany hookahs, they were led to the top deck, where everyone from dinner was lounging in a huge hot tub with a waterfall feature, and champagne flowed over a slab of smooth white marble. Soon after that, I joined them there, and the rest is history.

16

We slept a bit on the flight home. One hour before landing, our flight attendant said, "My boss said to give you anything you wanted and to send you off with your bags laden with all the wine and champagne you could carry." We shook our heads in protest, but she insisted and said, "Yes, I insist. Otherwise, I will have to take it home with me." What could we say? Then she asked us for our names. When we told her, she handed each of us a cellophane bag. Nestled inside each one was the iconic Tiffany's box the color of a blue robin's egg and smooth satin ribbons. As the city lights of Seattle drifted beneath us, Torey said, "One at a time?"

"No way," Jeanne said. "All of us together."

"I'm with Jeanne. On your marks, get set, *go!*" chimed Kat.

Each box contained a delicate bracelet encrusted with diamonds, rubies, sapphires, topazes, Hawaiian pearls, and a large emerald representing the earth. Blue sapphires were used to depict the oceans. A golden wings charm dangled from each bracelet, and there was an extra O-shaped ring to connect our golden dolphin charms. If I were a prince and could give such gifts, I would have wanted to do the same. We were speechless. Our names were printed on the cards, each of which read,

> Just a small token of our appreciation for an evening filled with genuine love, laughter, and affection. You were all a delightful sight to behold. Our world would be a better place if everyone treated one another with the love and respect shared by your group of friends. May your lives continue to be filled with dolphins and angels, and may you add the dolphins from your dentist next to the angel wings that we gift to you.

> In gratitude always,
> HRH and Carmen

We were nearly speechless. Jeanne had tears silently rolling down her freckled cheeks as she stared at her gift in awe and whispered, "I have never in my entire life or ever expected in my wildest of dreams to own such an exquisitely beautiful creation."

Kat piped in and said, "Carmen talked with me about the company she was starting. She wants to create beautiful, unique, one-of-a-kind pieces of jewelry. These must be from her line."

"How in the world could we ever express our gratitude for such a gift?" asked Torey. "I am astounded."

"Ya know," I said. "I think we already gave them a gift. We showed them a side of humans they don't normally see."

We helped one another attach our dolphin charms to our

glorious new bracelets and secure them around our wrists. "I am absolutely bedazzled," Ziggy murmured.

"Mm-hmm," we all responded.

We landed at Sea-Tac airport ahead of schedule. We wrapped our arms around one another's shoulders, mingled our tears, and said together, "I love you."

Feeling exhausted and weak-kneed, Jeanne mumbled, "Talk to you later."

I replied, "No, talk to you for the rest of our lives." And we climbed into separate taxies.

17

Upon our returning home, our lives resumed their normal, hectic pace. Torey moved her office to a larger space in a more prestigious location where she could hire more staff and acquire more accounts. Kat took on numerous million-dollar listings. Ziggy opened her own hair salon and started flipping houses. Jeanne was still overworked, but she had to keep the textile lines moving forward. Me? I returned home where life was moving swiftly along. My father was still reeling from the loss of my mom, and he'd just been diagnosed with prostate cancer, so we moved him into our house. I cared for my father, cleaned, cooked, drove teenagers here and there, gardened, and hosted parties at the ranch. I also dealt with a constant flow of teens who came and went from our house, which seemed more like a revolving door than a home at times. And I continued to work part-time in the emergency room. Looking back, our amazing adventure together felt like something unreal.

Though my friends and I missed one another, months passed without us seeing one another. We emailed as often as possible, always ending by saying, "Love you all. We really should get together for drinks and appetizers soon." From time to time, one of us would call to check in, decompress, and wonder aloud if it had all been a dream. The other would confirm it had all been real. We had experienced a lifetime of laughter, sadness, happiness, and so much awe in just a short space of time. It had been a once-in-a-lifetime experience—an experience that still had us shaking our heads about what could happen when least expected. Torey still said the experience had been more like a nightmare, yet she hadn't taken off her bracelet with the bejeweled angel wings and dolphin charms once, even to shower. When people commented on its beauty, she simply replied, "Don't ask. Suffice it to say that I received this from a prince who lives in a place far, far away."

One morning as I was lying in bed after Craig kissed me goodbye and the kids had gone off to school, the phone rang pulling me from my dreams. I reached across the sheets, which were still filled with Craig's warmth and scent, wondering who was calling before eight o'clock in the morning.

"Good morning," I mumbled groggily into the phone.

It was Linda, Jeanne's older sister. "What are you doing right now, Misha?" she asked.

"Huh? What d'ya mean? I'm still in bed."

With quivering breath, she replied, "She's gone."

"What? Who's gone?"

"She's gone," she repeated.

"What are you talking about? *Who* is gone?"

"Jeanne."

My world spun. Then a ringing started in my ears that would continue for several days. Jeanne's family said they hadn't heard from her in quite a while. So they started calling her, but she didn't answer or return their calls. After numerous failed attempts to get in touch, her sister went to her house. There she found Jeanne unconscious on her bathroom floor, covered in vomit, looking as if she had fallen and hit her head. She was alive but barely breathing. Her sister immediately called 911. The EMTs arrived within minutes and performed CPR all the way to the hospital, where she was immediately put on a ventilator. But it was too late. She had asphyxiated on her vomit. It had gotten into her lungs and deprived her of oxygen for too long.

"No!" I cried. "No, I don't believe it!" Jeanne's sister asked me to please come to the hospital right away as the family had decided to take Jeanne off life support. I wrapped my arms around my knees and rocked myself silently. Curling into the fetal position, I tried to imagine a world without Jeanne, but I couldn't. The tears came silently at first. Then they became loud and gasping, enough to scare me back into reality. I needed to talk with someone, but who would I call? Usually, I would call Jeanne when I needed comfort, love, direction, or any sort of guidance and understanding regarding big life changes or hardships. Her death didn't seem real, and I couldn't get a grasp on how I felt. I was in absolute denial, lost as to what to do.

Finally, I couldn't cry anymore and was feeling nauseated. I had to remind myself to breathe. The ringing in my ears wouldn't go away. I didn't know what to do. I closed my eyes, whispering her name over and over and over. When the tears tried to well back up, I squelched them, denying this was happening. Eventually, I picked up the phone to call Craig, but I realized I still wasn't ready to say the words out loud. I didn't want to move or talk to anyone or say the words out loud. It felt as if keeping them tucked deep inside would somehow stop it from being real. The warmth from Craig still lingered in the sheets on his side of the bed, I burrowed in seeking a semblance of comfort and breathing in his scent.

Eventually, I got up and dressed in a trance, trying to wrap my mind around what was happening. I knew I had to focus on just getting to the hospital. It was amazing what my body and mind were able to accomplish despite being in shock—driving the car, staying focused, shoving thoughts of losing my best friend out of my mind as soon as they tried to slip back in. Over and over, I thought, *I'm losing Jeanne. I'm losing Jeanne. No ... No ... Don't think. Just drive. Red lights. Green lights. Take the exit. Park the car.*

With each passing minute, my heartbeat continued to escalate until I could hear it pounding in my ears, rising up into my throat. I have no recollection of driving to the hospital, walking down the quiet hallways of the ICU, or reaching her room. She was in isolation, so I needed a gown, gloves, and a mask to enter her room. Her mother was with her, holding her right hand, head bowed down cross Jeanne's lap. She was hooked up to IVs, an intubation tube, EEG monitors, an EKG, a catheter, and a pulse O2 saturation reader—a weakening stream of beeping green and red lines. Her eyes were closed. She looked very peaceful, and her complexion was pink like she was sleeping a dreamless sleep. I could only stare, gulping back tears until a nurse came up behind me and placed her arm on my back. When she asked if I was a family member, I nodded numbly. Right at that moment, Jeanne's mom looked up and put her hand to her breast as if protecting her heart, and then she whispered my name. She carefully leaned over to kiss Jeanne's brow. Then she stripped off her gown and gloves, then with leaden feet shuffled out to me. As she enfolded me in her arms, just as she had done to Jeanne so many times before, I realized neither of us would ever be able to hug Jeanne again, a thought that wrenched my heart so violently I had to hold on to the windowsill to keep from crumbling. Jeanne's mother's arms wrapped around me, drawing me close to her own heart. It was such a soothing respite from the clatter and enormity of life's chaos. There, I found the tranquility and a safe haven where I could allow the grief and pain to come alive. In a mother's warm and loving embrace, as I sobbed silently, she held me closer, and we sobbed together, clutching each other as if that could somehow stop the inevitable. I was holding her up as much as she was holding me up. Connected by our love for Jeanne, our bodies formed a solid triangle as we held each other, hearts beating as one. After a while, she pulled away, saying she was going to find the rest of the family but that I should go ahead into the room to spend some time with Jeanne. She was so grateful that I was there. Knowing that Jeanne would feel me there eased her pain a little.

Filled with trepidation, my body felt like lead as I lifted my arms so that the nurse could assist me in putting on the gown and cap. I washed my hands and then walked over to Jeanne's bed. I picked up her hand, tracing each finger with my own. I was surprised that I seemed to know her hands as well as I knew my own. Her hands were so feminine, and she had the most perfect fingernails. I had envied her beautiful hands since junior high. There on her wrist I recognized the small scar she'd gotten as a little girl after falling from a swing set. I played "connect the dots" with her freckles and then kissed her palms and used her fingers to wipe my tears. As I stroked her cheeks with the backs of my hands, I started talking to her, reminiscing. Memories were coursing through my mind like a raging river. I laid my head down next to her face on the pillow as I talked, hearing the whoosh of the machines around us, knowing they were keeping her alive, there, with me.

From the very start of our relationship, Jeanne knew me better than I knew myself. She would finish my sentences for me before I had even thought through my responses. As a child, I learned how to create my own happiness as my mom and dad drank their bottles of Gallo wine and contended with six children and God only knew how many pets. It was tough as a middle child, lost in all the commotion, always trying to make peace. To top it all off, I was probably a little dyslexic with a touch of ADHD. When I first met Jeanne, I knew right off the bat that she was ADHD too. She was also the middle child in a family with alcoholic parents. We were the same size—me with long blonde hair and sparkling gray-blue eyes, her with long red hair and green cat eyes. We were definitely the cat's meow, and our energy as fifteen-year-olds could have filled the skies. Because we were both on the same wavelength—yakking to beat the band, unable to top each other's stories about who we were and who our families were—I loved her from the start.

One day shortly after we first met, she drove to my house in her daddy's big red convertible Cadillac with a cigarette between her lips. Spotting her, I came flying down to our mailbox and exclaimed, "God, are you crazy?!" I *never* would have driven a car without a driver's license, but she was my idol, so I jumped into the car with her, astounded at my bravery.

Another time I was babysitting for a lady who was Jeanne's neighbor, and I let my boyfriend drive her Camaro. (without his license) Jeanne agreed to stay home with the two little girls, after convincing my boyfriend and me to just take the car, which we ultimately did. We went to Woodland Park for a Fourth of July event. On the way home, he sideswiped a parked car, and I had to take the blame for it because I had the license and he, like Jeanne, was a few months younger than me.

If I came home with a new outfit on, I had usually borrowed it from Jeanne. Granted, she probably got it from JCPenney's, but that was still better than the hand-me-downs I got from my older sisters. Or it might have been an outfit that we stole from JCPenney's, where her dad happened to work as the manager.

We were also cheerleaders together in high school until I was kicked off—or "benched," as they called it—for wearing the same old fringe coat and grungy cords too many days in a row. Our cheerleading squad supervisor called me in one day and said, "Misha, you are a representative of the school, and the cheerleading squad advisers suggest you wear clothing more appropriate." Well, I must have been manic that day because I couldn't wait to spread the word and get all of our classmates in an uproar of support for me and my right to wear my old fringe coat and grungy cords. In an act of support, Jeanne voluntarily sat on the bench with me the rest of that school year, both of us wearing suede fringe jackets and corduroy bell bottom pants.

Another time I was benched for getting a D in geometry, even though I maintained As and Bs in all my other classes. *Sheesh,* I thought. *Gimme a break.* Fed up, I dropped off the squad. Poor Jeanne had joined the squad late in the game, and she was having a terrible time learning all the moves. So we both said *sayonara* to high school cheerleading and left that day, thumbing our noses, feeling pretty ballsy. After that, we started skipping classes and driving Jeanne's mom's little blue Datsun wherever we wanted.

One day we were driving an hour north of our little hometown, singing, smoking pot, and doing the Funky Chicken. Doing the Funky Chicken always led us to parties and fun in the north end of Seattle, Jeanne's old stomping grounds. Oh, the joy of being sixteen without a care in the world. There we were, driving down the road when all of a sudden, coming toward us from the opposite direction was Jeanne's mom on her way home early from work! We were far away from where we were supposed to be. Shit, we were busted. Jeanne waved. Furiously yelling and motioning for us to pull over, Jeanne's mom pulled over behind us. She sat in her car for a minute with her hand over her heart, head leaning back against the headrest, eyes closed. "Oh boy, this is it," Jeanne had said. "She's pulling the heart attack move. Just stay here. I have to go talk to her." Well, duh. Jeanne walked over to her mom's car and tapped on the half-open window. Her mom opened her eyes and shouted, "You follow me home *right now, young lady!*"

We had so much fun in those days—sharing clothes, sharing thoughts, sharing our lives, each of us becoming part of the greater whole. After high school we both bought old VW bugs. I began working for a dentist down the street from the grocery store where she worked. She would drop me off on her way to work, and then during her evening breaks, she would take me back home. It was so difficult for us to say goodbye to each other. It was as difficult as separating Siamese twins, we used to joke.

Jeanne married her high school sweetheart, and I moved to the other side of the state to live with my high school boyfriend. Jeanne had babies right about the time I met and started dating Craig. While I was falling in love, she was busy raising two young children, and we lost track of each other for a short spell. She was in my wedding though just as I had been in hers. When I became pregnant with our first child, Jeanne and I got back in touch, and it was like we had never been apart. We joined an all-women's soccer team and had the best time playing soccer for a summer. We shared the same ob-gyn, who doubled as our soccer coach. My water broke as I was talking to her on the phone. My husband and I bought property on Lost Lake, and Jeanne and her family often joined us.

There were times when I picked wild mushrooms while Jeanne shot chickens and chopped wood. There were also the times when we dressed up for Halloween. Jeanne was a devil in a red satin bodysuit. I was a "figment of your imagination" with glittery scarves and a silky ball gown. We sang and danced until dawn. One year we weaved ribbons of colored yarn together to make Christmas scarves. And there was the time when I put too much bubble bath in the hot tub and it overflowed, covering the whole deck!

I reminded her of the intense political discussions she and Craig used to have at the dinner table. She gave him the nickname "the Bulger" because his neck veins protruded so much when she got him riled up.

I helped Jeanne pack up and move everything out of her farmhouse one weekend while her husband was hunting. He had been verbally and physically abusing her just as her father had. She moved into the small cottage on our property and got a great job in the textile industry, and then she had an affair with her boss, who she later married. When they moved away to another state, she and I lost touch again until she eventually moved back.

I recounted for her a time shortly after my mom died where I was registered to be in a horse show in another state. I didn't want to go, but Jeanne reassured me that it was exactly what my mother would have wanted me to do. It was a regional event where I had to place first, second, or third in order to qualify for the US nationals. Not only had mom just died, but I had broken my leg in a camping accident and was still recovering from the mental and physical turmoil. Jeanne insisted I go to the horse show. She even offered to drive me there and stay with me for moral support since Craig had to stay home and care for the kids. Jeanne was not a horse person, but her love for me outweighed anything else. When I was in the warm-up arena, my trainer was yelling at me for holding the reins too tight or sitting wrong or putting too much pressure on my unbroken leg and not enough pressure on my injured leg. Out of the corner of my eye, I saw Jeanne crawling through the railings, traversing the whole outside of the arena, dodging horses and riders, and marching right up to my trainer. With a cigarette in her hand, she jabbed him in the chest, giving him a piece of her mind. She asked him where his sensitivity was and if he had any. Maybe he was just a lowlife cowboy and didn't care about anything I had just gone through in the last few weeks. He stood back and took it. Then he chuckled and respectfully escorted Jeanne out of the arena. The whole barn got a real laugh out of that. Oh, how we all had wanted to yell at him and give us a piece of our minds throughout the previous year of grueling training. Jeanne was my hero! I couldn't believe she had walked right up to him in that arena without any regard for the horses running around her.

I reminisced all of this and more, in whispers as she lay in the hospital bed, continuing to share each memory of our lives aloud as they entered my mind until I fell asleep only to be awakened by a nurse coming in to check on her vitals. She told me a few family members needed to go home to get some rest, but they had decided they were going to take her off the ventilator later that evening. There was always the miraculous possibility Jeanne would breathe on her own for a few hours or even days. "This would be very unlikely though," the nurse added softly. I stayed and talked to Jeanne more, massaging her feet, combing her hair, singing her songs, saying all the prayers I could think of, and literally trying to memorize every feature and count every freckle. I just couldn't let go. After a while, Jeanne's mom came in and told me to go home for a while and come back after supper. I couldn't imagine eating or drinking anything. I'd felt extremely nauseated ever since the call from Jeanne's sister that morning, which seemed like eons ago. When I remembered I had the keys to her house, I knew I had to go there first.

Despite having spent hours with Jeanne in the hospital, I had a difficult time pulling myself away and leaving her alone. I knew she never would have left me alone. To leave

MICHELE ETHIER

her was the most difficult decision of my life, knowing it would be our last time together. Even though I knew she had no brain activity, Jeanne was still so alive to me. I heard her voice and laughter in my ears. I felt her filling my heart to its fullest capacity. As I lied beside her, the silence of our stillness grew deafening. Slowly, I drew circles on her palm and then stretched her fingers wide open. She felt so warm with the heated blanket over her. When I brought her hand to my lips, I realized how cold I was. I trembled, and then I was suddenly overwhelmed by chills that washed over me in waves and coursed through my body. Something was happening that I had no control over, and I was trying so hard to stay with Jeanne, to let her know she wasn't alone. I was there with her. I also desperately wanted her to comfort me as she always had. What would I do without her?

I walked out of hospital, feeling numb, drained, empty, and so lost. I needed Jeanne to talk to me, to tell me what to do, to cry with me, and to laugh with me at this crucial, ludicrous time in our lives. Finally, I called Craig, but I broke down sobbing again. Trying to give me what little comfort he could over the phone in the middle of his workday, he said he would leave work early to go to Jeanne's house with me. But I needed to go alone. I needed to feel close to my friend. Jeanne's spirit lived within the walls of that house where we had spent so many loving times together watching movies, eating ice cream, drinking wine, chatting in the hot tub, making Christmas presents, and solving all life's problems. Then laughing hysterically, we'd set those aside and solve the world's problems. The memories cascaded over me, crashing down heavily one after the other. I just couldn't lose her. My heart was being dragged through a quagmire of unknown territory, and I had no idea how to navigate through it. The only thought that gave me any comfort was remembering that she loved me as I loved her—deeply, unconditionally, and eternally. Knowing this truth gave me the courage to keep going.

When I reached Jeanne's house, my legs felt like I had run a marathon. I could barely walk up the steps to her front door. As soon as I entered, I was rushed by sweet little Chewy. This precious kitty had given us so much love and had been through so much with all of us. I fell to the floor, gathered her in my arms, and buried my face in her soft fur. With Chewy purring in my arms, I collapsed onto the couch and began running my hands over the rich brocade. As I grabbed the blanket, that had most likely been wrapped around Jeanne just a day or so before, Chewy nuzzled my nose. She wrapped herself around my neck and lovingly bonked her head into my face. She was wearing a collar embedded with the crystals the Watsu therapist had given to Jeanne and me in Hawaii after our Watsu sessions. As I choked back my emotions at the sight of them, I felt completely spent and gone. I was exhausted, but I knew I needed to let Kat, Ziggy, Torey, and Layne know what had happened. On each call we cried together, but nothing they said could relieve me of this emptiness. We had no words and no answers. What do you say? A pool of tears had collected in the whorls of my ears, and I didn't even notice it until I stood up and felt them trickling down my neck like a free-flowing stream.

Suddenly, I was overtaken by a desperate need to walk through Jeanne's house—to touch, feel, and smell everything. There was no music, just the silence and the absence of Jeanne. As if in a dream, I traced her footsteps inside her home. I felt her more profoundly than ever before. I couldn't get enough. I was like a fish out of water, gulping and gasping in all the essence of Jeanne that I possibly could before returning to the hospital, before they took her off life support. I was terrified—more scared than I had ever been in my entire life. My heart leaped into my throat with every step. In the bathroom I found a towel, still wet, draped on the towel rack, her hair dryer sitting on the countertop, and her brush still filled with her golden-red hair. Half-chewed black-olive-and-pepperoni-pizza vomit covered the floor. Under her kitchen sink, I found rags, a bucket, and some bathroom cleaner.

After cleaning the bathroom, I went into the laundry room, picked up all the dirty clothes, and threw them in the wash. Then I emptied the dryer and folded the clean clothes. As the shadows outside lengthened, the sunrays took on a slant, and I cleaned the house like a maniac. In a frenzy I reached into the liquor cabinet and grabbed every bottle of wine, vodka, rum, and tequila, and then I loaded them into my car. I filled several trash bags with her empty wine bottles and tossed them into my trunk to discard at home. I added her vibrators to the stack of stuff in my car too. Like a mad woman, I began rummaging through her garbage, reading every scrap of paper, trying to hang onto any little thing Jeanne had touched in recent days before I threw it out. I stripped the bedding from her bed. I organized her closet and emptied her refrigerator of perishable items. As I went through the house, I felt like I was hoarding pieces of Jeanne, removing items that she wouldn't want her family to see. Throughout it all, Jeanne was with me, giving me comfort and guiding me toward the items I should remove to protect her family through their days of hardship.

I went outside as the afternoon sun descended behind the mountains and covered me in dusk. Then I walked the path Jeanne had made outside to her garage. After cutting pink roses from her garden, I arranged them in beautiful vases throughout her living room and bedroom. Our little Chewy was never far behind me, letting me pick her up to hold and love for brief escapes before I relapsed back into insanity mode over and over again. As I was figuring out what lights Jeanne would have wanted me to leave on, I remembered our

Hawaiian charm bracelets. I retraced my steps to her closet to find her jewelry box. There it was nestled within the blue velvet pouch along with some jewelry that she and I had made together in high school and a macaroni necklace one of her children had made for her. I also found her father's wedding band, the necklace she always wore with her green and purple dress, an assortment of earrings, gifts I had given her, and a beautiful pearl and emerald crucifix I had never seen her wear before. *How could that be?* I wondered. I pocketed her charm bracelet because I wanted to give it to her daughter personally sometime within the next few days.

I called Craig to tell him I would be heading back to the hospital after dropping by with Chewy first and breaking the news to our children. I was in a frantic space and just felt the need to get back with you as soon as I could. I crumbled when I saw Craig. He caught me and held me up as my sobs became lost and muffled in his warm chest. As he held me close and rocked me gently, we didn't say a word. I handed Chewy to him and told him to tell the kids, "Here is a gift from Jeanne." I just couldn't face them, and he would know the right words to tell them. He always did. Plus I didn't want them to see my pain, to see my crying, not yet. I was barely hanging on, and I had to stay strong for just a while longer.

When I returned to the hospital, everyone was there with Jeanne. Her mom was cradling her head, her sisters and brother surrounding her bedside, and her two children were rubbing her feet. Surprisingly, it all looked so peaceful. As I stood transfixed by Jeanne's face through the hospital room window, I realized how angelic she looked. The nurse came up behind me and whispered, "Would you like me to help you put on a gown so you can go in?"

"When are they removing the ventilator?" I asked just as a doctor arrived and started helping me with the gown.

"Right now," he answered.

My heart flipped and flopped so hard that my knees nearly buckled. I stood there shaking my head back and forth in denial. I was trying desperately to catch my breath, steady my breathing. This was not real. This is not really happening. *I'm sorry,* I told Jeanne, *but I just can't go in and witness this last chapter with you. I just can't. You have earned your wings, and I will feel you as my guardian angel every single day. Our love was boundless and eternal, which gives me some peace. I knew from the moment we met—me on my pony, you as the new kid to the neighborhood—you would be part of me always. In heaven, I believe there is no need for words. So when my days are finished, I await your greeting as I glide through the light that will bring us together as one once again.*

The nurse put her arm around my waist and offered me a glass of water. Pressing it to my lips, she said quietly, "Come over here and sit down." Then she led me to another room. As I walked through the doorway, the doctor pulled the curtains closed.

18

I believe that contributing to the well-being of others is fundamental to being human. Providing support and care to others has always been my passion in life. I thrive on guiding and teaching people to feel good about themselves. Is this my middle child syndrome rearing its head? Probably. As suggested by many scientific studies, I was predestined to be a peacemaker and caretaker because I was born smack dab in the middle of a family of six children.

As an adult, I was fortunate and blessed to be a stay-at-home mom. Taking care of my husband, and three children, has given me enormous satisfaction, pride, and peace. I was also able to care for my mother as she faced Lou Gehrig's disease, and when Jeanne left us I was doing the same for my father, who was living with progressing dementia. I also worked in the health field, caring for doctors, staff, and patients. Running my own health and fitness day spas where I could assist my clients in becoming the best they could be with proper nutrition, exercise, and detoxification gave me the opportunity to acknowledge myself, realize my passions, and live them even after my children left the nest.

My passion to enrich, teach, and support others in their lives wouldn't exist if I didn't feel rewarded by it. Caring for my husband and our three children, then both my ailing parents, seemed only natural. I was in my comfort zone and grateful to have found happiness in doing what I did. When women are under stress, it is not uncommon for them to care for others as a way of coping. I learned this coping technique as a little girl, and caring for others was what I had been doing my whole life. Of course, being needed by a multitude of people at the same time can produce stress rather than alleviate it. Fortunately, I did balance my priorities, which is a difficult task to accomplish even in the best of times.

Find purpose and passion in life. Strive earnestly and with focused intent. Passion is our emotional heartbeat. The longer we go through life without clarifying it and without seeking our purpose in this life, the less passion we will have. As we go through life, passion is what sustains us as we reach toward our goals. It can turn the impossible into the possible. Without it, our lives can be dull, drab, and boring.

The following words were written by a friend of mine named Molly. These words have always resonated deeply with me.

> To my guides and spirits and all those who are assisting me in my evolutionary journey on this earth—
> It is my intention that I experience a harmonious lifestyle.
> It is my intention that I experience health and energy that leads me to creative adventures.
> It is my intention that I experience love and that I give love out in all the things that I do.
> It is my intention that I have fun and laughter in my life on a daily basis.
> It is my intention that food and shelter and all the things I need to experience a happy life be given to me in great abundance and that I share this abundance with others.
> It is my intention that I do not become overly enamored by the material world.
> It is my intention that when I feel confused or divided, I have faith and patience until my way is clear. It is my intention that I fulfill my destiny and find my true purpose and sense of completion in this lifetime.

I have always strived to win the respect of intelligent people and the affection of children. I appreciate beauty and try to always see the best in others. I believe in giving of oneself to make the world a better place, whether by raising a healthy child, a content pet, or a beautiful flower or vegetable garden. I believe in playing, laughing with exuberant enthusiasm, and singing with reckless abandon. Knowing that even one life has breathed easier because of how I have chosen to *live* is what I believe it means to become a success in life.

All emotions are beautiful. Seize them. Bless them. Know they are part of you. We all are in our own sea of confusion, at once ashamed and proud of what we have seen and experienced, heard, and witnessed ... or of what we haven't seen and heard, what we haven't done.

After losing Jeanne, my friendships with other women took on a deeper meaning. We all are human beings first and foremost. Our similarities are as vast as the sky, and we all love and hate. We all feel sadness and happiness in much the same ways. Both birth and death bring forth undeniable emotions that are difficult to express with mere words. We all were once newborn infants fresh from heaven, unmolded yet ever changing. We *all* are the same. Once we love ourselves, we will see how effortless it becomes to love everyone else.

When my husband and I returned to Hawaii the following year, we met up with the dolphin swimmer and Watsu instructor. One afternoon as the sun was descending behind the horizon, she and I kayaked out to the rim of the bay where we had encountered the family of dolphins once before. We paused, and I rested my chin on my knees before tossing a lei into the waves. I uncorked a small vial of Jeanne's ashes and poured them into my palm, and there was a whisper of a breeze as I slowly let them sift through the creases and inlets of my fingers. My tears slid down my chin, joining the beautiful blue waters of the sea.

That evening I was holding hands with Craig and walking along the black sand beach, imagining myself as a magi reaching into the folds of my velvet cloak and pulling out handfuls of glittering silver crystals. I tossed them high, allowing the trade winds to capture their essence so that they could be added to the star-strewn skies. I have heard that the stars are actually our loved ones who have passed away, watching over us now. I believe it. I will continue making wishes on shooting stars. Forever.

THE END

Signs and Symptoms
of Inner Peace

- a tendency to think and act spontaneously rather than fears based on past life experiences
- an unmistakable ability to enjoy each moment
- a loss of interest in judging the self
- a loss of interest in interpreting the actions of others
- a loss of interest in conflict
- a loss of the ability to worry
- frequent and overwhelming episodes of appreciation
- contented feelings of connectedness with others and nature
- frequent attacks of smiling
- an increasing tendency to let things happen rather than make them happen
- an increased susceptibility to the love extended by others
- an uncontrollable urge to extend that love

To begin, you must learn about yourself, who you really are. Most importantly, be honest with yourself. In truthfulness, you can respect yourself and others. If something hurts or bothers you, you can't ignore it or lie to yourself that it's really "not all that bad." It will always be there and possibly haunt you in the future. It's hard on the soul to live with restrictions and doubt. You'll find yourself trapped, not knowing which way to turn. At times you think things are getting so rough you need a friend to help you. Friends can listen and give reassurance, which might be all you really need. Still, whatever the problem is, the way you handle it is ultimately your decision. Be at peace with yourself. Strive to make life an enjoyment. What is best for you is what is most important. You have to live with yourself for the rest of your life, and amid all the confusion and turmoil that life can bring, you can always seek refuge in yourself.

Guardian Angels

The belief in guardian angels can be traced throughout time. Pagans, including Menander and Plutarch, and Neoplatonists, such as Plotinus, held this belief. The Babylonians and Assyrians also held the same belief. The figure of a guardian angel that once decorated an Assyrian palace is now displayed in the British Museum. Nabopolassar, father of Nebuchadnezzar the Great, said, "He (Marduk) sent a tutelary deity (cherub) of grace to go at my side; in everything that I did, he made my work to succeed."

According to Leo Trepp, the belief developed in late Judaism that "people have a heavenly representative, a guardian angel. Every human being has a guardian angel." Rabbinic literature frequently expresses the notion that there are indeed guardian angels that watch over people. God watches over mankind and makes decisions directly connected with their prayers. In this context, the guardian angels are sent as emissaries to aid in this task. Thus, we don't pray to them directly, but they are involved in the workings of how responses to our prayers come. Rashi comments on Daniel 10:7, "Our sages of blessed memory said that although a person does not see something of which he is terrified, his guardian angel, who is in heaven, does see it; therefore, he becomes terrified."

Jean Daniélou writes in his classic study of Jewish

Christianity that later theology borrowed the doctrine of the guardian angel for Jewish Christianity. He says that Clement of Alexandria writes in the *Eclogae Propheticae* that according to scripture, little children are entrusted to guardian angels who bring them up and make them grow. And they shall be, he says, "like the faithful here who are a hundred years old" (XLI. 1). As reported in Mathew 18:10, Christ said, "See that you despise not one of these little ones: for I say to you, that their angels in heaven always see the face of my Father who is in heaven." This is often understood to mean that children are protected by guardian angels, and this assertion appears to be corroborated by Hebrews 1:14, which says, "Are they not all ministering spirits, sent forth to minister for them who shall be heirs of salvation?" According to St. Jerome, the concept of guardian angels is in the "mind of the Church." He said, "How great the dignity of the soul, since each one has from his birth an angel commissioned to guard it."

In Acts 12:12–15, there is another allusion to the belief that a specific angel is assigned to protect each individual. After Peter was escorted out of prison by an angel, he went to the home of Mary, the mother of John. The servant girl Rhoda recognized his voice and ran back to tell the group that Peter was there. However, the group replied, "It must be his angel" (Acts 12:15). Peter's angel was the most commonly depicted guardian angel in art, most famously shown in Raphael's fresco of the *Deliverance of Saint Peter*, which presently graces the Vatican.

In Genesis 18–19, angels not only act as the executors of God's wrath against the cities of the plain, but they deliver Lot from danger too. In Exodus 32:34, God says to Moses, "My angel shall go before thee." At a much later period, we hear the story of Tobias, which might serve as a commentary on the words of Psalm 91:11, which says, "For he will command his angels concerning you to guard you in all your ways" (Cf. Psalm 33:8 and 34:5).

The guardian angel concept is clearly present in the Old Testament, and its development is well marked. The Old Testament conceived of God's angels as His ministers who carried out His behests and who were at times given special commissions regarding men and mundane affairs. In the New Testament, guardian angels work as the intermediaries between God and man. A key example from the New Testament is the angel who comforted Christ in the Garden of Gethsemane (scene 3).

The belief that angels can be guides and intercessors for humans can be found in Job 33:23–6, and in Daniel 10:13, angels seem to be assigned to certain nations. In this latter case, the "prince of the Persian kingdom" contends with Gabriel. In the same verse, Michael is termed as "one of the chief princes." See Deuteronomy 32:8 (Septuagint) and Ecclesiasticus 17:17 (Septuagint). In the book of Jude, Michael is described as an archangel. Scripture says that God will "set a guard of holy angels over all the righteous "to guard them during the end of time.

Among the first of the Christian theologians to outline a specific scheme for guardian angels was Honorius of Autun. In the twelfth century, he said that every soul is assigned a guardian angel the moment it enters a body. Scholastic theologians augmented and ordered the taxonomy of angelic guardians. Thomas Aquinas agreed with Honorius and believed that it was the lowest order of angels who served as guardians, and his view was most successful in popular thought; however, Duns Scotus said that any angel is bound by duty, authority, and obedience to the divine authority to accept the mission to which that angel is assigned.

Centuries later in his 1997 Regina Caeli address, Pope John Paul II referred to the concept of guardian angels twice and concluded the address with the following statement: "Let us invoke the Queen of angels and saints, that she may grant us, supported by our guardian angels, to be authentic witnesses to the Lord's paschal mystery."

Christian mystics have reported ongoing interactions and conversations with their guardian angels, sometimes lasting years. Saint Gemma Galgani and Maria Valtorta are two examples, both having also reported extensive visions of Jesus and Mary. Saint Gemma Galgani was a Roman Catholic mystic who interacted with and spoke to her guardian angel. She stated that her guardian angel acted as her teacher and guide, at times stopping her from speaking up at inappropriate moments. The bedridden Italian writer and mystic Maria Valtorta wrote *The Book of Azariah* based on dictations that she directly attributed to her guardian angel, Azariah.

Additional Information on Watsu

Watsu is currently provided in many international health and wellness spas as well as in some aquatic physiotherapy programs. It is finding countless applications in therapy, aiding recovery from injury, relieving muscular and joint pain, and encouraging movement and flexibility. In addition, many are enjoying sharing Watsu's simpler moves with family and friends. At practitioner level, it can stand alone as a therapy or be used as a wonderful complement to therapeutic work on land.

Many clients will come with a specific focus (e.g., pain syndromes, healing after injury or surgery, specific movement restrictions, etc.), while others seek Watsu for the feelings of relaxation, blissful surrender, time away, and quiet meditative stillness that it can induce.

Imagine the warmth and sense of weightlessness induced by water. Your eyes are closed, so there is just the play of light across your eyelids. Your ears are underwater, so the sound of the world is muffled. The world starts to disappear, leaving just you and your experience being in the water with nothing to do, nowhere to go. You are just receiving and letting go into the graceful rocking, cradling, and gentle rhythm. It is no wonder people speak of states of bliss and levels of relaxation never before imagined. You feel a boundless joy, tranquility, and peace meandering through you senses. You find the rhythm of your own heartbeat.

Specific therapeutic effects noted by receivers include increased mobility and flexibility, muscle relaxation, fuller and deeper breathing, reduction in anxiety and stress levels, decreased pain, improved sleep and digestion, and a general sense of well-being.

Each person's experience is unique and varied. For many, the focus will be on the physical effects of letting go, relaxing, stretching, and freeing the spine and joints. Others might experience emotions, new personal insights, or the resurfacing of old memories. Many receivers will remark on the deep sense of beauty or lightness, ease, and grace experienced during their Watsu, or they will talk about a sense of nurturing, safety, relaxation, maybe at a level never felt before or one remembered from long ago. The way Watsu is experienced is as varied as individuals themselves, so there is no right or wrong way to receive it. Practitioners do not push any particular aspect but simply listen and support the receiver's experiences in each session.

The Water Watsu Girl

Tender and yet tantalizing,
Even somewhat hypnotizing,
Reaching for your deepest feelings,
Rendering amazing healings,
Yet you can't depend on finding dolphins when you need
unwinding.

Watsu is the perfect answer
And makes your heart a dancer,
Lifts your spirits, soothes your tension,
Keeps you floating in suspension,
Emulating dolphins drifting.
Rarely can life be more uplifting.

—Glen Ethier (Misha's father)

Spinner Dolphin Facts (Stenella longirostris)

People are fascinated with the spinner dolphin. They are one of the most social of all species. They are also one of the most spectacular to see in the wild, thanks to their amazing jumps, flips, and spins outside of the water.

Description

Spinner dolphins are small and slender. Their size will vary based on where they reside. Commonly dark gray on their backs and light gray on their sides, they are known for their white bellies. They may also have a very dark gray stripe running from their eyes to their flippers. They have long thin beaks with a triangular dorsal fin.

The average size for a spinner dolphin is six to seven feet in length, and they usually weigh between 130 and 170 pounds. The males are longer and heavier than the females. The males also have a more distinctive post anal hump than the females, and they also have smaller heads. A dwarf subspecies of the spinner dolphin has been identified around the southeastern portion of Asia.

Distribution

Most spinner dolphins are found in the open oceans of the tropics. They tend to live farther from land than most other species of dolphins. They are known to live in various oceans around the world, including the Pacific, Atlantic, and Indian. They may be found looking for food in shallow waters from time to time. In Hawaii, they have been seen closer to the coast than in any other region. They will rest in the bay areas for protection during the day.

Behavior

Spinning in the air is the characteristic behavior of the spinner dolphin. These famous jumps and spins typically take place at night. Spinner dolphins are also known to ride in the wakes or bow waves of boats. These playful mammals live in groups that range from one hundred to more than one thousand. Within the larger pods, there are many complex but smaller pods with a definite hierarchical structure. They are extremely social within their pods, as well as with other species of dolphins. They have been seen using echolocation to find one another. They also touch frequently and create very close bonds.

Resting at various inlets is a common practice during the day for spinner dolphins. It is common to see them returning to the same locations day after day. After they have rested and the sun has started setting, they soon get busy looking for food. Migration is another big part of life for these dolphins. They move long distances to follow prey and to stay in warm waters.

Feeding

Squid is a huge part of the spinner dolphin diet. They have no problem successfully hunting in the deeper and darker waters of the ocean, yet squid are more apt to come to the surface of the water at night. These dolphins are rarely seen feeding during the daylight hours. They also consume large amounts of fish and shrimp. Most of the time, they dine on vertically migrating species. They can dive up to 984 feet to get food.

Reproduction

Females are ready to mate around four to seven years of age. For males, it occurs later, specifically between seven and ten years old. Their mating rituals have been observed by researchers. They tend to touch often and to pay plenty of attention to the ones they plan to mate with. The time of year for mating depends on where the dolphins live geographically. Many believe that there are only a couple of times a year when hormone levels increase and mating occurs. After mating, it takes about ten months for a calf to arrive. The mature females give birth once approximately every three years. The young will be born tail first, which is the case with all dolphins. They will grow very quickly, consuming milk from their mothers. They will be completely weaned at about two years of age. They will be introduced to other food sources at around six months of age though. The bonds between a mother and her young can last a lifetime. The average life span in the wild for spinner dolphins is twenty years.

Conservation Status and Threats

At this time, they are considered to be an endangered species because of the effects of pollution and diminishing habitats. So too, many are injured or killed in fishing nets. Stress caused by human activities in their environment can create health problems in spinner dolphins as well. Pollutants, such as chemicals and plastics, in the water have also become a major concern.

There are some conservation efforts in place for spinner dolphins. One of them involves better equipment for fishing that would reduce the number of them getting tangled up in nets. Some of the fishing commercial entities follow these dolphins to find tuna, and that increases the risk of them getting caught as well. The Dolphin Safe program in the United States has helped in this area.

Many have considered ways of reducing stress in the environment as a result of boats and other elements. Reducing such threats is important, but it can also prove to be very tricky. In areas of Hawaii, some have researched how limiting where people can go during the day could help. Many believed that the sleep of the dolphins resting there was frequently interrupted by humans during the day, causing them a great deal of stress.

Efforts to reduce pollution have been a primary focus for conservation. One of the threats that we must still address is the hunting of them for sport or for meat in countries outside of the United States. Even though there are some efforts in motion to prevent such hunting, such activities do indeed occur on a wide spectrum. It is hard to enforce these laws and provide protection from such hunting in many regions.

Excerpt from "How to Swim with Dolphins: A Guide to Being" Author Terry Walker

Earth mission involving human hearts
Universal time: Now
Earth time: 1950

The group leader spoke to the pods for the last time before takeoff. After checking logistics and pod assignment coordinates, he announced the pod mind's intention of a successful and fulfilled mission. Everyone already knew that by heart. It had been the first step in a long process that was culminating with them flying to earth to assist humans in their evolution.

Humans had this ridiculously mistaken notion that *might made right*, and because they were on the verge of stepping into space, it was determined (by the council for universal balance) that it was time for guidance. It was easy enough to infiltrate the cetacean organisms that already lived on earth. Those who had volunteered in previous times during their numerous earth endeavors had good covers. They had also made human contacts, and the timing was perfect to escalate these.

It was time that humans discovered the power and energy of love. The pods had the ability to transmit straight from the heart the light and energy to stimulate transformation at the deepest levels of the human psyche. All humans craved love. (It was the bottom line for all their actions and endless reactions.) They would be drawn to the oceans to receive it.

To reach those humans who might never make it to the oceans, there was a special elite pod. They would allow themselves to be taken from the oceans and placed in small stone swimming ponds where landlocked humans would come to them. It was the most risky and dangerous part of the mission, but it allowed for more human contact. The ocean pods maintained constant telepathic contact with those taken to keep their hearts clear and spirits strong. The potential for abuse by humans in these situations was very high. It was the primary job of scattered subgroups throughout the oceans to maintain the connection with these captured ones at all times and beyond. Eventually, as all flowed according to plan, a consciousness of *one heart* would be established on earth. The mission is going exactly as intended. Awareness is always the key to a heart.

TRUE DIRECTIONS

An affiliate of Tarcher Perigee

OUR MISSION

Tarcher Perigee's mission has always been to publish books that contain great ideas. Why? Because:

GREAT LIVES BEGIN WITH GREAT IDEAS

At Tarcher Perigee, we recognize that many talented authors, speakers, educators, and thought-leaders share this mission and deserve to be published – many more than Tarcher Perigee can reasonably publish ourselves. True Directions is ideal for authors and books that increase awareness, raise consciousness, and inspire others to live their ideals and passions.

Like Tarcher Perigee, True Directions books are designed to do three things: inspire, inform, and motivate.

Thus, True Directions is an ideal way for these important voices to bring their messages of hope, healing, and help to the world.

Every book published by True Directions– whether it is non-fiction, memoir, novel, poetry or children's book – continues Tarcher Perigee's mission to publish works that bring positive change in the world. We invite you to join our mission.

For more information, see the True Directions website:

www.iUniverse.com/TrueDirections/SignUp

Be a part of Tarcher Perigee's community to bring positive change in this world! See exclusive author videos, discover new and exciting books, learn about upcoming events, connect with author blogs and websites, and more!
www.tarcherbooks.com

TRUE DIRECTIONS
AN AFFILIATE OF TARCHER PERIGEE

Made in the USA
Lexington, KY
24 August 2019